"Ready to be surprised?"

She rolled her eyes. "I guess I have to be."

"You're going to love it," he said. He kissed her on the cheek, then led her into the backyard. Michael was all smiles when she saw the fire pit glowing and the food on the table. But it was the telescope that caught her eye.

"What's this?"

"Some people call it dinner." Jamal's arms went around her waist. "Shrimp, grilled peppers and hush puppies. Because I know you love them."

"Really? I can't lie—they are pretty awesome. And I have dessert. Shoot, I left it in the car."

"We can have it for breakfast."

"Breakfast? You assume I'm spending the night?"

"Not assuming, just stating a fact. I plan to keep you up all night."

Michael blinked and her mouth fell open. Images of her body pressed against Jamal's naked one flashed in her head. "I didn't come here to sleep with you, and if…"

"Whoa, little red Corvette, slow down. While I would never kick you out of bed, tonight i̶s̶ ̶d̶i̶f̶f̶e̶r̶e̶n̶t̶." Jamal pointed to the telesc̶o̶p̶e̶ ̶a̶n̶d̶ ̶s̶a̶i̶d̶ ̶I̶ ̶w̶a̶n̶t̶ ̶t̶o̶ give you the universe.

Dear Reader,

Sometimes you never know what you need until she or he smiles in your face. Jamal Carver didn't know he needed one woman to love until Michael "MJ" Jane came into his life. Convincing her that he's willing to give up his playboy ways will take some effort, because MJ will not be played, no matter how much she finds herself falling for this sexy former marine.

Writing about two people who were looking for anything but love was a fun journey, and I hope you will enjoy the heat.

Always,

Cheris Hodges

THE HEAT
Between Us

CHERIS HODGES

HARLEQUIN® KIMANI™ ROMANCE

Recycling programs
for this product may
not exist in your area.

ISBN-13: 978-0-373-86519-2

The Heat Between Us

For questions and comments about the quality of this book please contact us
at CustomerService@Harlequin.com.

HARLEQUIN®
www.Harlequin.com

Printed in U.S.A.

Cheris Hodges was bit by the writing bug early. The 1999 graduate of Johnson C. Smith University is a freelance journalist and always looks for love stories in the most unusual places. She lives in Charlotte, North Carolina, where she is trying and failing to develop a green thumb.

Books by Cheris Hodges

Harlequin Kimani Romance

Blissful Summer with Lisa Marie Perry
Feel the Heat
The Heat Between Us

This book is dedicated to my readers.
Without your support, I'd probably be wondering what
to do with all of these stories floating around in my head.
Thank you for allowing me to share them with you!

Chapter 1

Michael Jane, also known as MJ, yawned as she leaned back in her office chair while reading over the latest edition of the local newspaper. It wasn't that the story was boring—she just hated Monday mornings, and this one was particularly difficult. Mimi had talked her into a three-mile run, and then a green smoothie for breakfast.

No wonder the caramel beauty was tired and ready for a power nap. MJ looked at her reflection in her compact mirror. Her light brown eyes were sparkling and her auburn curls were actually in perfect form today, despite her run this morning. MJ was often complimented on her full lips, especially when she smiled. It was the one trait she'd got from her mother that she appreciated. Her lips and the beauty mark near her bottom lip.

"Miss Jane," her assistant said. "You have a visitor."

"Who is it?" Michael stifled another yawn. She knew she didn't have any appointments this morning, which was the only reason she'd allowed Mimi to talk her into that crazy run.

"Nicolas Prince."

Michael groaned and tugged at her auburn tresses. "Send him in."

Before the door opened, Michael smoothed the corners of her mouth then sat up straight in her chair.

Nicolas Prince used to be the man of her dreams, the man she'd seen standing at the altar on her wedding day. Now he was simply the client she wished she'd never signed to her marketing company. Nic, who'd always had a healthy dose of confidence, leaned on the strength of their friendship to show up without an appointment. It wasn't a good look.

"Good morning, beautiful," he said as he walked in and took a seat in front of her desk.

"What do you want, Nic?" She sighed and ran her fingers through her hair. MJ played with her bouncy curls when she was annoyed. Nic's unannounced visit was very annoying. Granted, there was a time when seeing Nic would've sent her heart fluttering and made her smile. She'd even gone so far as to fantasize about a future with him. But that was before he'd made it clear that he didn't have the same feelings for her that she had for him, leaving her crushed. Nic had used her to get what he wanted and she vowed that she'd never be used by another man again. Mimi Collins-Daniels, MJ's best friend, had tried to warn her that Nic was a player, but Michael had wanted to see the best in him. She wanted to believe that she could be the one to bring out the love in him, like a princess in a fairy tale. Unfortunately, life wasn't a fairy tale and neither was her one-sided relationship with Nic.

At least she'd learned her lesson. She'd never make the mistake of falling for a player again.

"What's up with the attitude this morning?"

"Why are you here without an appointment? Mondays are busy days for me." She raised her right eyebrow. "You could've at least brought coffee and bagels if you were going to come in here unannounced."

Nic shook his head. "Well, I apologize, but I have an amazing idea and I need your help to make it sizzle."

MJ sighed. "I'm listening."

"Are you?" He rolled his eyes. "Stayed out partying last night?"

Michael gave him a look. "Get on with it. I have another appointment." The sooner he said what he had to say, the quicker she could get him out of her office. "And how I spend my nights aren't your concern. What's your idea?"

"The Great Atlanta Jazz Fest. A two-day citywide event to spotlight the growing scene here and give New Orleans a little competition."

MJ perked up in her seat. "Go on."

"Of course my spot would get the most publicity because I'd be a main sponsor and host all of the after-parties."

Michael gave him an icy glance. "Yeah, I imagine you would expect that. What about the artists?"

"I have a few ideas. A few of the groups I've had at the club would be great headliners. But we need some big names."

"Okay, so how are we going to work this event and get the city on board?"

Nic nodded. Michael turned to her computer and pulled up her internet browser. "We need to make sure we don't have any of the same artists who were in New Orleans headlining here. We want Atlanta's jazz fest to be different, our own thing."

Even if this festival was Nic's idea, MJ knew having her company attached to a successful event like this would put her business at the top when it came to landing multimillion-dollar accounts. She needed this to work, even if it meant working with Nic.

Nic slapped the edge of her desk with excitement. "And this is why I came to you. I knew you could make this work. You're one of the only other people I know who can take an idea and make it as big as it needs to be."

"Me and my staff..."

"No, MJ, I'm only working with you on this. I know your people are sharp, but you're the best."

"Everyone here is capable of making this a stellar—"

He interrupted her. "We have a contract, remember? It says that we—"

"Clearly, I know what it says," she snapped. "Give me a couple of days to get a proposal together. Then we can start firming up plans."

"Miss Jane," her assistant said over the intercom. "Mimi Collins is here for you."

Nic rose to his feet. "My cue to leave. I'll call you to make an appointment so that we can go over this in more detail."

"Please do," she replied as Mimi walked in.

There was no love lost between Michael's best friend and Nic. Ever since they were undergrads at Spelman and Morehouse, Mimi and Nic had butted heads. MJ could never put her finger on why, and at this point she'd chalked it up as one of life's unexplained mysteries.

"Ooh," Mimi said, giving Nic a cool glance. "Am I, hopefully, interrupting something?"

"Hello and goodbye, Mimi. I was just leaving." Nic strode to the door.

"Don't let me stop you." Mimi took the seat that Nic had vacated.

"Guys, this is my office, not the quad," Michael said. "Nic, we'll talk soon."

Mimi made a face and crossed her legs as Nic walked out the door. "Please tell me that was about business."

"It was and you're rude!" MJ broke out into laughter. "I don't get you two."

"Whatever. Are you in as much pain as I am?"

"Not you, Miss Marathon Queen." MJ rolled her eyes. "Let me just go on record and remind you that this morning's run was your idea."

Mimi yawned. "Well, I had a bit of a workout last night with my loving husband, so three miles was a bit much this morning." Mimi stretched her left foot out. "And these heels are murderous. But I had to show up at the Blog-Her conference looking like a million bucks."

"Umm, TMI, Mimi! How's the conference going so

far?" Michael asked, quickly changing the subject. MJ had watched her friend rise to fame and infamy with the power of the keystroke as the creator of the *Mis-Adventures of Mimi* blog. After her public spat with the online dating website *Fast Love*, Mimi had fallen in love with her attorney, Brent Daniels. Michael had hoped their real love story would've made her friend a little less controversial on her blog. It hadn't and that was why the public loved her. Mimi still wrote about relationships and real life issues.

Her last post had been about women not waiting for a man's potential to kick in while dating. The post had gotten over seven million hits.

"I think I might have started something positive," Mimi said with a smirk.

"Why does that statement scare me?"

"Because you're nuts. I met a web designer who wants to make a site that celebrates women. Highlights our trials and tribulations. Falls from grace and comebacks. There are a few sisters looking to create some dating apps that aren't just about your looks and can match couples by the books they've read."

"That does sound positive. I could see myself logging on to an app like that." MJ smiled. "And what else has been going on at the conference?"

Mimi smiled and excitement sparkled in her eyes. "A lot of good ideas in our early sessions. There's even talk of a *No More Mistresses* website that would list all of the married men pretending to be single on dating websites." Mimi kicked off her shoes. "Enough about me. Why was Nic here?"

"Business. He wants to do a citywide jazz fest and

I'd be handling the marketing for it. We're just sketching things out right now. But it sounds like it could be a great idea."

"I hope it's successful for your sake. But Nic can hug and kiss my—"

"Got it, Mimi."

"I forgot to tell you this morning, but Jamal asked about you over dinner."

MJ smiled and Mimi pointed at her. "What?"

"You and Jamal. What's that all about?"

MJ sucked her teeth. "Jamal and I are just friends. He's a foodie, despite the fact that he looks like he eats nothing but protein bars. We were going out Saturday night, but I got a call from a client because of some negative social-media reviews. We had brunch Sunday morning. Then he had to set up security at a venue for a concert or something."

"So, this thing with you and Jamal is still light and fun or…"

"Stop it. Because for the last time, we're just friends." And Michael wondered if they would ever be more than that. If she was honest with herself, she'd admit that she wanted to be more than Jamal's friend, but she also knew his reputation as a ladies' man, so she kept her heart as guarded as possible. The last thing she would be was another name on his list of conquests. And she wasn't about to get her heart smashed again by expecting too much from a man who didn't know what he wanted.

Jamal loved his family, especially his grandmother Ethel. Every Monday, she called him to make sure he was taking care of himself—as if he was a teenager away at boarding school. And every Monday, he looked forward to his early morning conversations with his beloved grandmother.

But at this moment, he needed to get off the phone. A blast from his not-so-distant past had just made eye contact with him.

"Gran, I have to go," he said as he saw a woman walking toward him with a smile on her face. How was it that the one morning he decided to go out for breakfast, he ran into Loony Lu-Lu, also known as Lucy Becker? The wannabe Atlanta socialite couldn't fathom that Jamal rejected her advances and she couldn't take no for an answer. And she always seemed to show up out of nowhere like a ghost of bad dates past. Jamal had gone out with Lucy only once. They'd attended a concert where she spent most of the night on her phone Tweeting and taking selfies for Instagram. It was a boring date, and when she outlined her plans for being on a reality show, Jamal knew he'd never go out with that crazy bird again.

Too bad she hadn't gotten the message.

"Jamal, I do wish you would settle down like Brent. Look at him and Mimi, just as happy as they can be," Ethel said.

"Gran, how do you know that they're happy?"

"Because I read her blog! Anyway, go ahead and do whatever it is you said that you had to do and make sure you get me some fresh crawfish for my Savannah boil this year. I know that stuff you brought last year was frozen."

Jamal chuckled, surprised that his grandmother read Mimi's saucy blog. He remembered how Brent had gotten all out of sorts when his wife had written about their kiss on that infamous blog. "All right, Gran, fresh crawfish and settle down like Brent. I'm going to give you a call tomorrow." He disconnected the call and bit back a groan. If Jamal thought he was going to get away from Lu-Lu, he was wrong.

"Jamal Carver," she exclaimed, "you could've invited me to breakfast and I would've gladly accepted. Now you had to eat alone and where is the fun in that?"

"Hello, Lucy. Being alone is always fun—best company ever." He wiped his mouth with a napkin and dropped it on the table. Rising to his feet, Jamal reached for his wallet and left enough cash to pay for his breakfast and tip his waitress. "Well, I'm off to work. Have a nice day," he said.

"How about we have a nice night, together?"

"I'm good," he said then headed for the door. Jamal silently cursed himself out for ever going out with Loony. He'd known his lips were dangerous, but he'd kissed her anyway. And she'd fallen head over heels. If only he had that effect on Michael Jane's sexy ass.

Sighing, he unlocked his Ford Mustang and slid behind the wheel. MJ had been the star of his dreams since they'd met at his buddy's cookout last year. Despite her masculine name, Michael was all woman, with dangerous curves he wanted to ride like the wind. And those expressive brown eyes. Sometimes, he'd just stare at her to watch the golden flecks in them. MJ's dimples were another reason why he'd always tried to make the caramel beauty smile.

But she had wanted to keep things light. Normally, he'd be all for that, but something about MJ made him look for more. Was his gran right about it being time to settle down?

When he arrived at his security firm in the heart of downtown Atlanta, he focused on the breakdown in coverage at a concert his firm was providing security for where a deadly shooting had happened. He needed answers and someone was going to lose their job today. Jamal prided himself and his company on keeping people safe. His reputation wasn't going to be sullied by people not doing their jobs. And then there was always the possibility of a lawsuit.

Better call Brent after this meeting, he thought. Jamal walked into the conference room and looked around at his staff. Three of the men had been with him for a decade, and two of the guys had come highly recommended from his marine buddy, Walter Ramirez.

"What in the hell happened last night?" Jamal demanded.

"J," Harry Mancini began, "I was in charge last night and I take full responsibility for what happened. Around twelve thirty, the crowd started clearing out and I let two of the guys go home. Then the rest of us had to do security detail for the talent. We had no idea that there had been an argument."

"How did a weapon get on the premises? We were supposed to be checking cars as well! Did you guys not pat folks down?" Jamal asked, disappointed that he was going to have to let Harry go. But he'd dropped the ball big-time.

"We were, but…"

"No buts, Harry. What happened last night was unacceptable and you were in charge. A life was lost. I have no choice but to let you go."

Gasps filled the room, but Jamal wasn't finished. "The rest of you are off duty until further notice. I can't have people on my team who don't follow the rules. We're the First Line of Defense and last night we were worse than rent-a-cops."

Harry rose to his feet and headed for the door. "Jamal, I'm sorry about what happened, but these guys don't deserve this punishment."

"And that's not your choice to make."

Jamal waited for the men to file out of the room before he dropped his head on the table. What he did had to be done but it still wasn't easy to do. Pulling out his cell phone, he called Brent.

"What's up, Jamal?" Brent asked when he answered.

"I'm in trouble," Jamal began. "Or potentially in trouble."

"What's her name?"

"Bruh, this is serious. First Line of Defense was the security company at that concert over the weekend."

"Oh, shit. And people are talking about suing you already?"

"No, but it's only a matter of time. This is America and after the tragedy comes the lawsuit."

"Yeah, but they will probably go after the promoter and the artist first. That's where the money is."

"Still, my guys failed to do their job and I feel responsible."

"Don't say that to anyone else. I know you take your job seriously and you have an impeccable reputation, but you can't save everybody and no one is going to hold you responsible."

"That's what you say until someone files a lawsuit."

"If they do, then you know I got your back. Stop borrowing trouble."

"You're right, but I had one of my top guys running the point on this concert and I had to fire him today."

"Damn, that was harsh."

"So was not following my rules. But whatever. I'm going to go do some paperwork."

"Dude, this is not like you at all. What's the real problem?"

MJ.

"Who said I had a problem?"

"Your actions and your attitude. The last time I saw you act like this was during the… What's her name?"

Jamal groaned. "It's MJ."

"I knew it. I thought you guys were just kicking it and having a good time?"

"And I thought I could handle that," Jamal said. "Any other woman, I would've been good with that, but there is something different about Michael."

"Yeah, she doesn't want you. Forbidden fruit is always the sweetest."

"Says the man who married his former client. I guess you would know."

"I'm going to chalk that up to you not getting any and being jealous. You know nothing happened between Mimi and me before I settled her case. Not that it matters now, because she's my wife and whatever I did worked."

"I know. As a matter of fact, I should send your wife a few dozen roses to get her to help me win MJ over."

Brent broke out into laughter. "You know if you ask Mimi for help, you might end up fodder for her blog."

"Umm, I forgot about that. You know my gran reads her blog. Still, I don't know how and why Michael has gotten under my skin the way she has," Jamal said. "I feel like I'm one step away from being Loony Lu-Lu."

"Is that woman still after you?"

"Sadly. Like they say, it's the ones you don't want who are always chasing after you."

"That's what happens when you have too many ones," Brent said. "I got to go, but I can tell you this— I might be having lunch with my wife and her best friend at the new Sunshine Café in the West End around one thirty."

"You might be getting a six-pack of craft beer to relax with this weekend. I'll see y'all at one thirty," Jamal said.

After hanging up the phone with Brent, Jamal felt a little better about everything.

He glanced at the clock on the wall and realized that he had too much time on his hands to sit there and think about Michael. So, he logged on to his computer and pulled up his rules-of-engagement document for his employees and printed it out. He didn't want any more excuses about not knowing what to do.

Chapter 2

Michael and Mimi were still sitting in her office when Brent called his wife. As she listened to Mimi cooing and laughing into the phone, Michael could only shake her head. But she had to admit, love looked really good on her friend. She couldn't believe she'd ever thought that a narcissist like Nic was capable of making her feel like this. *Get over it.* Turning to her computer, she googled the lineup for the past New Orleans jazz fest and made notes of the artists who had performed there. She wanted to make sure they didn't book the same people for the Atlanta event. Then an idea hit her. What if they used local bands? That would really give the Peach City its own thing. The food would have to be amazing as well. She then started searching some of the restaurants that Jamal had introduced her to that she enjoyed. As she thought about her dinner with him last week, she couldn't help but laugh. They had been sitting on the patio at a new Peachtree Street eatery when a woman walked over to Jamal and threw a glass of water in his face.

She'd gone off on him for not returning her phone calls and proceeded to call him every name in the book. Then Jamal had dried his face with a napkin and stood up and handed her a dollar.

"Maybe this will help you buy a clue as to why I didn't call."

It had been funny to Michael, even as a part of her wondered if this was what it would be like dating a playboy like Jamal.

But they *weren't* dating.

"What are you giggling about?" Mimi asked as she dropped her phone in her purse.

"Nothing as exciting as whatever Brent was saying to you."

"He was reminding me that we shouldn't be late for lunch." The smile on her friend's face told Michael that was not all he'd said. "Come on, MJ. Leave those files and let's get moving. You know how traffic is around here."

"Yeah. But you're driving since you made me run this morning."

"And we're running tomorrow as well, so get ready for it."

Michael groaned as she rose to her feet. "I never thought I'd say this, but I can't wait for you to go back to New Orleans."

"Whatever. You know you miss me when I'm not here. And luckily for you, once my travel series is over, I'll be back in Atlanta full-time. That means we can run every morning."

"No, ma'am."

Mimi rose to her feet and told her friend that she and Brent would see her at the restaurant in about an hour. Before MJ could tell her friend goodbye, her phone rang.

Monday was actually turning into a busy day for her.

Finally, after she wrapped up her calls and reports for her clients about their marketing campaigns, it was time for lunch.

If it hadn't been for the fact that Michael had been clamoring to try the new West End restaurant, Sunshine Café, she wouldn't have agreed to be the third wheel on Brent and Mimi's lunch date. She started to tell her friend not to become that married woman who was always trying to hook up her single friends.

Mimi and Brent were the perfect couple, in her opinion. He was the calm where Mimi was the storm and it worked for them. Her friendship with Jamal was a bit like that. The more time they spent together, the more she found things to really like about him.

The fact that he was a foodie and found the most off-the-beaten-path restaurants in the city always made her smile. She hoped that she could introduce him to a place for a change.

If only he wasn't such a playboy…

Walking into the restaurant, she smiled when she saw Mimi waving for her. "Brent got held up on a case at work," she said when Michael made it to the table. "This place seems really nice."

"I know. I was hoping to tell Jamal about it, since he is always finding cool places for us to eat around the city."

Mimi laughed. "Were you expecting him for lunch? Because here he comes."

Michael turned toward the door and smiled when she saw him walking her way. Their eyes locked and Michael's heart rate increased. *Relax*, she told herself.

Jamal Carver was a beautiful, yet rugged, man. His caramel-brown skin was smooth as silk and that goatee gave him the right mix of tough and sexy. His bedroom eyes gave hints of mystery and sex, and that brilliant smile just made her melt every time. Even if she tried to deny there was an attraction between them that went beyond friendship.

Then he had a body that seemed chiseled from mythological marble and wood, crafted by a sensual deity for pleasure and desire. But since she wasn't the friends-with-benefits type, she kept her wanton thoughts under wraps.

"Hello, ladies," he said when he reached the table, then leaned in and gave Michael a kiss on the cheek.

Mimi smiled. "Jamal, what are you doing here?"

"Thought I'd check this place out and I see that great minds think alike," he said then winked at Michael as he took a seat across from her.

"And here I was hoping to scope it out and bring you someplace new for a change," Michael replied.

"Have you all ordered yet?" Jamal asked.

"No, and I'm going to go," Mimi said as she waved her phone, a peculiar gleam in her eye. "Brent wants me to meet him at the office."

Jamal and Michael shared knowing glances. "Umm, huh," Michael said. "I bet he doesn't need you."

"Anyway. You two enjoy—lunch, that is," Mimi said as she rose to her feet and sauntered away.

"Were we set up or what?" Michael asked.

Jamal shrugged innocently. "I have no idea what you're talking about. You know how I love new restaurants."

"Sure you do," she quipped. "How's your Monday going?"

"It just got a thousand times better," he said with a wink. Michael felt herself blush.

"Glad I could help," she said. "Hopefully this place is as good as it smells."

Jamal reached across the table and took her hand in his. "What are you doing tonight? I have something I want to show you."

"What?"

"Why would I tell you now?" He stroked the back of her hand with his thumb. Shivers of delight attacked her spine as his fingers caressed her. It wasn't as if he hadn't held her hand before, but today felt different. She slipped her hand from underneath his, urging her heart to return to its normal pace.

"Because I hate surprises."

"Too bad. About nine, meet me at my place."

"Jamal, I... Okay."

"Don't get all excited on me," he quipped.

"Oh, stop," she said with a giggle.

A few moments later, a waitress appeared at the table to go over the day's specials. Michael decided to go with the shrimp, chicken and grits, while Jamal was a bit more adventurous and chose a crawfish jambalaya pie.

"Wow," Michael said. "Now, that was a bold choice."

"Have to try it first to see if I don't like it."

She nodded in agreement. "But if you don't, my grits are so off-limits."

"Just selfish. But I'm sure this food is going to be amazing. If not, I have good company."

"Flattery is not going to get you a spoonful of my grits," she joked. Michael liked being with him—laughing was so easy. But she couldn't and didn't want to risk her heart again or get hurt. Jamal was everything that she knew wasn't good for her. A playboy. Would he even want to settle down with one woman? Could he?

"MJ?" Jamal said, breaking into her thoughts.

"Yes?"

"Where did your mind go?"

"Work. A client who came in today wants to do a citywide jazz fest."

"Mmm, that could be a logistics nightmare, depending on how many venues you plan to use."

"Not when I know a dream team that can help." Michael smiled. "First Line of Defense, perhaps."

"I'd be happy to help, but I have to be honest with you. We had an incident over the weekend."

"What happened?"

He told her about the shooting at the concert and

how his team hadn't been able to prevent it. "Ten years in business and nothing like this had ever happened."

"People make mistakes, Jamal."

"But this is bigger than a mistake. Someone died."

"And that's not your fault."

"Wish I felt that way," he said as the waitress made her way to the table with their food.

Jamal was silent until he and MJ took their first bite of food. Then they were singing the praises of the dishes and Jamal wasn't thinking of last night's tragedy. "These are the best grits I've ever had!"

Jamal nodded in agreement. "And the corn bread is tender and sweet. Reminds me of something else."

She rolled her eyes. "And what would that be?"

"You."

"Jamal, you probably say that to all of the girls." Michael wiped her mouth with her napkin.

"Being that you're the first girl I've eaten with here, you're the only one who gets treated to this."

"For now."

"This is officially going to be our spot. It's going to be MJ and Jamal's, not the Sunshine Café. Should I carve our names in the table right now?"

She hid her grin as she shook her head. "You're a mess."

"And? If I was Joe Regular, you wouldn't be here with me, now would you?"

She smiled and nodded. "You're right. And that pie looks delicious."

"It is." Jamal held a fork full of his savory meal out

to her. When Michael closed her lips around the fork, he was jealous. That fork had what he wanted. Michael's lips and tongue. Then Michael moaned. He could make her moan like that. She just needed to give him the chance.

"So good."

Jamal nodded. "Like I said, this is our spot. And for the record, I want points for sharing my food."

She nodded. "Ten points for sharing your food. Only if the dessert is as good as the entrées."

Jamal slowly allowed his eyes to roam over Michael's lithe body. "Where does it all go?"

"What?"

"The food."

"Burns off in the gym. You should join me for one of my morning workouts."

Jamal laughed. "You're not ready. Have you forgotten that I'm a marine?"

"Sounds like you're challenging me and I'm always up for a challenge. You haven't learned from that spades game at Brent's place?"

"Yeah, but you won't have your partner in crime Mimi this time. Name the time and the place."

"Six a.m., Anytime Fitness in midtown."

"Hope you like burpees."

Michael rolled her eyes. "I'm the burpee queen. Hope you like losing."

"Want to know a secret? Brent and I let you ladies win that day because he wanted to get in Mimi's pants."

"That's bull and you know it. Brent was going to get

into her pants win or lose. When you guys want a re-match, we're not hard to find."

Why did she have to say "hard"? Thinking about her in a pair of spandex shorts and a sports bra made him harder than a brick. "I hear you talking, beautiful. But this time we will show no mercy. Brent already has his woman." *And soon enough, I'm going to get mine.*

"And just like Mimi, I don't like to lose." Michael winked at him then waved for the waitress.

"Yes, ma'am?" she asked as she approached the table.

"Do you have a dessert menu?"

"Of course. I'll bring it right over to you."

Michael looked at Jamal with a smile on her lips. "I hope they have chocolate cake."

"With lots of icing." He winked at her, and then his cell phone rang. When he saw Brent's name, he started to ignore it, but he excused himself from the table and took the call.

Michael watched as Jamal walked away, talking on the phone. Part of her wondered if it was one of his women. *This is stupid. If I can't trust him, why am I here?*

The waitress returned to the table and handed her a menu. "Is that your man? Because, girl, you are lucky."

"Oh, we're just friends."

The waitress's mouth dropped open. "Does he know that?"

"Well aware. Question—do you guys have a choco-late cake?"

She nodded excitedly. "And it is very good. Moist, and the icing is homemade."

"I need two big slices."

The waitress nodded and smiled as Jamal walked back toward the table. "He has the hots for you," she whispered to Michael. "You better take advantage of it before I do."

Michael offered her a mock salute. "I'll take that under advisement."

Jamal sat down and placed his hand on top of Michael's. "Sorry about that."

"No worries."

"That was Brent. He had news for me about the shooting this past weekend. So far, it looks as if we have a legal standing if lawsuits start piling up because the promoter should've…"

Michael threw her hand up. "You don't have to explain anything to me. You get phone calls."

Jamal shook his head then polished off the last of his pie. "Did you find anything you liked on the dessert menu?"

"Oh, yeah. I think it's coming our way right now." She nodded toward the waitress.

"That's some good-looking cake," he said as the waitress set the hunking slices on the table.

"Just wait until you taste it." The waitress gave Jamal a wink and Michael felt a twinge of jealousy. Was this woman really flirting with him in front of her face? But then again, she'd just told her that she and Jamal were only friends.

"You wouldn't happen to have any milk, would you?" Michael asked, wanting to send her away.

"Soy, almond or regular?"

"Definitely almond with a side of ice."

The waitress turned to Jamal. "Can I get you some milk as well?"

"No, just some water." When the waitress left, Jamal took a glance at Michael as she took a big bite of her cake slice. "I know you aren't going to eat all of that."

She stuffed it in her mouth and smiled. "Mmm."

Jamal followed her lead and took a big bite of the cake as well. It was good, but when he saw a drop of chocolate on Michael's bottom lip, he didn't care about how the cake tasted because he wanted to taste her.

"What?"

Jamal leaned forward and wiped the chocolate from her lip with his thumb. "Just a drop of chocolate on your face."

Chapter 3

Michael shivered at the feel of Jamal's thumb against her lip. Something about his touch just made her body tingle. She wanted him, but knew it probably wasn't a smart thing to want. Playboys were like leopards—their spots didn't change simply because you wanted them to.

"Th-thanks," she said.

"No problem. Got to keep that pretty face clean. Or you could've used that shot to market this cake."

"They haven't hired me yet, so no free advertising."

"You're hard-core, huh?" He stuck his finger in the chocolate icing and brushed it across her full bottom lip. Just as he was about to lean in and kiss the confection away, Michael beat him to it and licked the chocolate herself.

"Okay, this icing is so good that I would give them a shout-out for free."

"How nice of you," he said. "Don't forget to meet me at nine tonight."

"For a surprise, right?"

Jamal kissed her hand. "Yes. And, no, I'm not telling you what it is. But I do have to run. I have a meeting in the heart of the city and I'm about to be late."

"Have a good meeting and I guess I will see you tonight."

"Come on—you can't act like that."

"Here's the second surprise—if I show up or not. And you should probably save your seduction skills for someone else." MJ nodded toward the waitress who was clearing a table not far from theirs. "She'd like it, I'm sure."

Jamal pulled out his wallet and left enough cash on the table to pay for their meals. "You think I'm trying to seduce you?"

She rolled her eyes. "You're telling me that you're not?"

"Babe, if I was trying to seduce you, you'd be in my arms right now. Just make sure you're not late tonight." He winked at her then headed for the door.

Michael watched him walk away and realized that he was right. She'd see him at nine, and no matter what his surprise was, she was going to enjoy it. Be happy about it and pretend that it didn't make her heart and soul melt.

"I'm in so much trouble," she muttered as the waitress walked over with her glass of milk.

* * *

Jamal hopped into his car and drove to the Atlanta Metro Credit Union. He was meeting with the head of security there to revamp their security protocol. As he walked into the building, his mind was on MJ's lips. That woman wore that chocolate like the most delicious lipstick. He'd wanted nothing more than to kiss her and taste that sweetness on her. But she was faster than he'd expected and had licked the chocolate away.

Seeing her tongue pass over that full bottom lip had made his blood pressure rise off the charts. What was it about this woman that made him want her so badly? Maybe it was because she told him no or the fact that she didn't act like the typical Atlanta women he'd dated. She didn't think that three dates meant they were in a relationship or that the fifth date meant an engagement ring was coming next.

MJ was the exact opposite. She didn't take herself, or what they had going on, seriously. At first, he'd enjoyed it. Felt as if he could be himself around her. He could be silly. He could be serious. They could talk politics in one sitting then turn around and debate about who the best comedian of all time was. Jamal had never found that range of conversation with another woman.

And the woman liked football. When he'd scored two tickets to the Atlanta Falcons season opener, he'd taken MJ with him and she'd been an avid fan of the game. Especially the star cornerback. Jamal had been impressed because most women he'd taken to a game knew only the quarterback and maybe a wide receiver or two.

"Defense wins championships, and the way Atlanta looks right now, we're going to the big game!" Michael had said at the end of the game.

"It's just the first game of the season."

"You have no faith."

"I know we have Carolina twice this season and their offense is finally as explosive as their defense," he'd said.

"Please. We're going to eat them up."

Smiling at the memory, Jamal walked up to the receptionist and asked for Craig Franklin.

Michael returned to her office and decided to throw herself into work. She didn't want to think about Jamal, but in the silence of her office, all she could do was think about him. If his finger was any indication, his kiss would be damn near deadly. Shivering, she wondered if anything would happen beyond the heat between them. Would the fire burn out and she end up like the woman who tossed that drink in Jamal's face?

"Nope. I'm not going to let that happen." Logging on to her computer, Michael did immerse herself in her work for about thirty minutes, and then her phone rang. When she saw Mimi's number, she answered because she was going to give her BFF a small piece of her mind.

"You're not slick, Mimi."

"What are you talking about? I had to meet my husband."

"Sure you did. You and Brent aren't slick at all."

"I had no idea that Jamal was going to show up at

lunch. That was all Brent because he said his boy was having a bad day."

"And I'm supposed to be the make-him-feel-better girl?"

"It worked, didn't it? I don't get you two."

"Wait a minute! You were totally against me getting serious with Jamal and called him a rebound."

"And you said you guys weren't serious." Michael could imagine her friend's eyebrow raised to the heavens. "So, what's the problem here?"

"We're friends, Mimi. Just friends. I don't understand why people don't get that. And I'm not looking for another dead-end relationship that is going to end up with me looking like a fool again."

"You like him more than you want to admit. Michael, remember the words of wisdom you used to give me? Time to take your own advice. Stop running and go after what your heart wants."

Michael rolled her eyes. "Because you took my advice, Mimi?"

"Umm, well, had I listened to you about that *Fast Love* post, I would've never had the chance to get close to Brent and fall in love with him. And you wouldn't have met Jamal. Then you'd still be sitting here pining for Nic."

"That's not true."

"What part isn't true? You meeting Jamal or still trying to show Nic that you're in love with him."

"Let's put Nic in the past, where he belongs. I wasted a lot of time trying to make him think we should've been a power couple. I own that. I'm over that."

"Then why are you working with him?"

"Contract."

Mimi sucked her teeth. "So."

"And if this event is as big as I want it to be, this is going to mean more high-profile clients, more big events and the success I've been chasing."

"You're already successful. You run this city," Mimi said.

"From your mouth to God's ear. People know I'm Mimi's friend, but they have no idea what I can really do."

"Whatever. How was the food at the café, though?"

"Amazing, and the dessert was superb. Maybe you and Brent should go there for dinner, since you guys set up that bogus lunch."

"For the record, it didn't start that way, but if you must blame someone, blame Mr. Law and Order. He told Jamal where we were having lunch."

"Oh, there you go. Let me tell you something, Mimi Collins-Daniels. If I read your blog and see any parts of me and Jamal on there, I'm going to hurt you."

"You mean like real names?"

"Don't play with me, Mimi!"

"All right, I'll try."

Michael sighed. "You better do more than try."

"You have my word, unless something really juicy happens. And don't say anything else, because I do write about myself on my blog."

"What does that have to…? Mimi, my brand isn't like yours, and if you…"

"Let me stop playing with you. I won't do it. And you better be ready to run in the morning."

Michael grinned. "About that run. I'm going to work out with Jamal in the morning."

"Ooh. With or without clothes?"

"Stop it. We're going to the gym. And he wants me to come see him tonight."

"You mean he wants to go on a date?"

"It's not a date. It's a…"

"D-A-T-E! Stop living in the land of denial. You two are getting to be annoying."

"Spoken like someone who has been annoying for years."

"And on that note, I'm hanging up."

"I love you, Mimi," Michael said through her laughter. After hanging up, she opened a file on her computer and started planning logistics for the jazz festival. When she typed in *security*, the only company she could think of to handle the job was First Line of Defense. Michael picked up the phone and called Jamal.

Voice mail.

"Jamal, this is MJ. Give me a call when you get a chance. I have a proposal, a business proposal, for you. I wanted to discuss it with you before I see you tonight, if possible. Thanks."

Jamal shook hands with Craig Franklin. "You've been really lucky," Jamal told the bank CEO.

"And I don't want to continue to press my luck. Your security ideas are just what we need to make the bank more secure from inside and outside jobs."

"You also shouldn't give an employee access to the video system. Not saying that you have someone stealing from you, but you have to be proactive instead of reactive."

"Makes sense. I look forward to your report and I'm sure the board will agree to the project."

Jamal nodded. "Let me know when you guys want me to get started and I'll send my tech team in."

The two men walked to the lobby and shook hands again. "Looking forward to working with you," Craig said.

Jamal nodded and told his client goodbye. When his phone vibrated in his pocket, he pulled it out and smiled when he saw a missed call and voice mail from MJ. If she was trying to back out of his surprise evening, he was not going to allow it. Tonight, he'd show her a side of him no other woman had ever seen.

Once he got into the car, Jamal listened to Michael's message. *Business proposal? Interesting*, he thought as he called her back.

"Hey, Jamal. I hope you got my message." Michael's voice was like a sweet song that he wanted to keep on Repeat.

"I did. Do you want to meet tomorrow and talk about it?"

"Aren't we getting together tonight?"

"Just looked at my watch and First Line of Defense is closed."

"Jamal."

"MJ. Listen, you do too much. Tonight, we're going to relax and not say a word about your proposal."

"All right. But you are considering it, right?"

"I'll tell you in the morning. When's a good time for us to get together?"

He could hear the keys on her computer moving at a rapid pace. "I have an opening at nine forty-five."

"That's about the time I have breakfast. Want to see if the Sunshine Café has better eggs than West Egg?"

"No, but I'll meet you at West Egg because those potatoes are just amazing."

"Good. See you later," he said.

"And what are we doing tonight?"

"You'll see when you get there. 'Bye, MJ."

Looking at her phone, Michael couldn't help but smile when she and Jamal hung up. He always made her smile. But that doubtful voice in her head kept telling her that they would never be serious. He was a player. And what made her think that she could be the woman who would change his mind about his lifestyle? The last thing she wanted was to be another one of those women who saw him out on the town and had an emotional breakdown.

That's not my style, she thought as she shut her computer down and prepared to leave the office. It wasn't easy to keep saying and pretending that she didn't want more from him. She just couldn't say it to him. Fear froze her tongue every time she tried. As she walked out of the office toward her car, she decided to head to the gym to burn off some nervous energy.

Would tonight be the night that she and Jamal took the next step in their relationship?

What was this big surprise? She knew that he wasn't going to propose. That thought made her laugh. It wasn't as if they'd known each other long enough for her to start fantasizing about being Mrs. Carver. She put the blame squarely on Mimi's shoulders for making marriage look so good.

As she pulled into the parking lot of the gym, Michael's cell phone rang. She wasn't happy at all when she saw Nic's name flash across the screen. She started to ignore the call, but she knew he wouldn't stop calling because obviously he needed something.

"Yes, Nic."

"Don't sound so excited. I just wanted to see if you had time to meet with me tomorrow. I have some great ideas that I want us to look at for the jazz festival."

"You do realize that it is way after office hours, right?"

"Since when did we start standing on ceremony?" Nic's laughter actually made her blood boil.

"Nic, you're simply a client. We aren't in a space where you can call me in the middle of the night because you have an idea. You made it clear that we're all about business. So, respect me enough not to invade my personal time because you have a freaking idea."

"I'm sorry—am I interrupting you and Mimi talking about whatever it is you two cackle about when you get together?"

"No, you're interrupting me and a very handsome man making a beeline between my thighs. Good night."

She ended the call and tossed the phone in the glove compartment. Michael was ready to punch something really hard now.

It was times like this when Jamal was glad he lived out in the burbs. Tonight he'd have a clear view of the sky and he had a fire pit that he didn't have to worry about getting zoning permission to light. He took his telescope to the edge of the woods that abutted his property and gave him the clearest view of the sky. Not many people knew that Jamal was an astronomy nerd. Since he was a kid, he'd enjoyed looking to the stars for answers. He would've been an astronaut if the *Challenger* incident hadn't scarred him. But still, he enjoyed watching the universe. And though he wouldn't tell his boys, he was a man who wished on stars sometimes. Especially when he was in Iraq. He'd prayed and wished for all of his comrades to make it through the night. He'd prayed and wished that the people he shot in the heat of battle were terrorists and not human shields.

The stars calmed him, made him feel as if he'd have his normal life back. After two years in the Middle East and an injury that left him unfit for combat, Jamal had lost partial sight in his right eye. And though he had surgery to correct the injury and remove the shrapnel from his eye, he hadn't been able to pass the physical requirements of the Marines to rejoin the corps. For about a year, he'd been a recruiter in Alabama. But Jamal missed action. Missed helping people and saving lives.

Deciding not to reenlist, Jamal had moved back to Atlanta and opened First Line of Defense. His grandmother had not been pleased. The matriarch of the Carver family wanted her only grandson, at the time, out of harm's way. She needed him to settle down and carry on the family name. For years, he'd ignored her constant nagging about finding the one. Jamal wasn't interested in a family. His father was MIA and that had had a huge impact on his life. He'd watched his mother cry over this man who'd broken his promises. One thing that Jamal could say about the women he dated was that he never made promises to them. He tried not to play with their emotions and make them believe that he was going to provide them a future.

In all these years he'd taken three women to his family's annual low-country boil in Savannah, but he now knew it had been a mistake to take any of them there. Introducing a woman to his family was unfair to her if he wasn't serious about the relationship, so Jamal had decided that the next woman he took to Savannah would be the one he planned a future with. And for a long time, he'd felt he wouldn't be bringing anyone down there for a while.

But lately, Jamal had caught himself wondering what it would be like to take MJ to Savannah. Would she even want to go with him this year? He figured that she'd say no. But he liked the idea of Gran and the family meeting her. He wouldn't even step in if they started asking uncomfortable questions like *Are you guys serious?*

That was a question he wanted an answer to. Could they be serious? What was holding her back from being his? Glancing at his watch, Jamal saw that he needed to get the shrimp on the grill and grab the graham crackers for the s'mores. Tonight was going to be simple and fun. And he hoped that it would lead to MJ understanding that he wanted her and no one else. She was a woman who made him feel like love did exist, without cameras and tabloid headlines. Too many women in Atlanta wanted to live like reality-TV stars. He wasn't about that life and he was glad that MJ felt the same way.

Even though she might not believe he was ready to be a one-woman man. But Jamal was so ready for MJ to be the only woman in his life.

Chapter 4

Michael stood under the cool shower spray after her hour-and-a-half workout. She'd hit the heavy bag, run for three miles on the treadmill and flipped a 350-pound tire thirty times. She was sore and tired. She wanted to call Jamal and see if they could reschedule, but she wanted to see him. She was excited about his surprise. Closing her eyes, she imagined him slipping in behind her, his big hands stroking her breasts until her nipples were rock-hard. Leaning her head back underneath the shower spray, she slipped her hand between her thighs, imagining that her fingers were Jamal's tongue. Hearing a throaty moan escape her mouth, Michael snapped back to reality.

Shutting the water off, she grabbed her towel and dried off. *Lord, grant me self-control when I see this man.*

After getting dressed in her favorite purple romper and silver sandals, Michael decided to get a surprise for Jamal as well. She drove to the Sunshine Café and ordered two slices of the sinfully delicious chocolate cake. She waved at her favorite waitress as the latter crossed the full dining room to greet her.

"Cake, huh? Where is Mr. He-Is-Just-My-Friend?"

"I'm taking this cake to him, because friends do stuff like that." Michael smiled.

"Umm, my mama would say that you're working on getting to his heart through his stomach. Good job. But you better learn how to cook, if you don't know how to already."

Michael broke out into laughter. "I'm so not after his heart and I can cook."

"And Shakespeare would say, *the lady doth protest too much*. Girl, if you don't jump on that man, I know a bunch of women in Atlanta who will."

Michael held her tongue because she knew a bunch of women in Atlanta already had. *How am I any different?*

"Well? I hope you have a thong and a cute bra on underneath that outfit." She wiggled her eyebrows.

"Not at all," Michael said. "Just friends."

"Keep in mind that we do cater weddings."

Michael took her slices and shook her head. "You're worse than my friend Mimi. Sounds like something she'd say on her blog."

"As in Mimi Collins? You know her."

"Yep."

"Tell her I'm her biggest fan. I comment on her blog as Cheyenne twelve-eighteen."

"I will let her know and maybe even bring her back for lunch tomorrow." Michael winked at her then headed out the door. Glancing at her watch, she saw that she was going to be late if traffic was bad.

For once, it wasn't. She arrived at Jamal's house right on time. She loved the quietness in his neighborhood. No sounds from the highway, no blaring horns and sirens every five minutes. And his lawn was always amazing. The little girl in her wanted to kick off her shoes and run through the manicured grass.

"Hello, beautiful."

She locked eyes with Jamal, who met her at the door dressed in a pair of cargo shorts and a white tank top. He looked so delicious and youthful as well as sexy. "Hey, you." He enveloped her in his arms and she inhaled sharply. He smelled good, woodsy and clean.

"Ready to be surprised?"

She rolled her eyes. "I guess I have to be."

"You're going to love it," he said. Kissing her on the cheek, he led her into the backyard. Michael was all smiles when she saw the fire pit glowing and the food on the table. But it was the telescope that caught her eye.

"What's this?"

"Some people call it dinner." Jamal's arms went around her waist. "Shrimp, grilled peppers and hush puppies. Because I know you love them."

"Really? I can't lie—they are pretty awesome. And I have dessert. Shoot, I left it in the car."

"We can have it for breakfast."

"Breakfast? You assume I'm spending the night."

"Not assuming, just stating a fact. I plan to keep you up all night."

Michael blinked and her mouth fell open. Images of her body pressed against Jamal's naked one flashed in her head. "I didn't come here to sleep with you, and if…"

"Whoa, little red Corvette, slow down. While I would never kick you out of bed, tonight isn't the night." Jamal pointed to the telescope. "Tonight, I'm going to give you the universe."

"The universe, huh?"

"First, we eat." Jamal led her to the table and pulled the chair out for her like a perfect gentleman. "And you can tell me what you have against surprises."

"What do you know about astronomy?" Michael asked as she dug into her shrimp. "And I don't like surprises because most of the time, it turns out to be something bad."

"That's because you haven't had the right kind of surprises. Stick with me, baby girl, and every day will be a happy surprise."

"I hear you talking. You're going to have to show and prove. I'm curious, though. How did you get into all of this?"

"I'm what you'd call a nerd—a sexy nerd, but a nerd nonetheless. When I was a kid, I'd always escape into the stars."

"Did you ever find anything up there?"

"Sometimes I did. But my big dream was to fly to the moon."

"Yet you joined the Marines and went to war?"

Jamal shrugged as he stabbed at his shrimp. "What can I say? I wanted to serve my country and I don't regret a minute of it. But when they get that space shuttle ready for commercial flights, I'm going to be the first one on it. Play your cards right and I might take you with me."

Michael almost choked on her juicy shrimp. "I'll watch you from down here while you shoot for the moon."

Jamal handed her a glass of wine. "Where's your sense of adventure?"

"Planted right here on the ground."

"Chicken."

Nodding, Michael took a sip of wine then set her glass on the table. "I'll be that. But I don't want to leave the Earth's atmosphere."

Jamal watched MJ eat her shrimp and his loins ached as he imagined her lips wrapped around him like that. Her tongue gliding across his hardness the way she licked the garlic sauce from the jumbo shrimp. He shifted in his seat, growing harder than a brick while watching her eat. He couldn't remember the last time the simple act of a woman eating had aroused him so much.

"This is so good."

"I bet you are."

"What?"

"Thank you."

"Who taught you how to cook?"

"My gran. She doesn't believe any Carver, male or

female, should be unable to feed themselves. So, when she went in the kitchen, she grabbed one of us to be her assistant. Then there was a quiz."

"Your gran seems like she doesn't play."

"She doesn't. You guys would probably get along famously."

"You think so?"

Jamal nodded. "We do a low-country boil at the end of the summer, when the whole clan goes down to Savannah. We all have a part of the meal we're responsible for. I'm the crawfish king."

"Sounds like fun. My family does catering and indoor reunions, once every five years."

Jamal popped a shrimp in his mouth. "You and your family aren't close?"

She shrugged. "We're busy and a small group, so... I guess we're not close. Mimi and I decided to make our own family."

"Y'all are very close."

"That's my crazy sister."

"She's mine, too, but always remember you and I are not related." He poured them both more wine. "Come on—let me take you to the moon." They walked over to the telescope and Jamal pointed to the pillows underneath the stand. "Don't take this the wrong way, but get on your knees."

Michael sucked her teeth. "You know..."

"I'm not the one with the dirty mind, baby. That's you."

She laughed and followed his directions. Then he wrapped his arms around her waist as he knelt behind her. "Now, if you turn your head to the left, you will see Orion."

Michael looked to the left with the telescope. "Wow. Now, is this the same as Orion's Belt?"

"That's the top of the constellation. But look at the whole thing. That's the thing about stars. When you look beyond the surface you see so much more."

She turned around and looked at him. "Why can't people be that easy?"

"People are that easy, if you take a deeper look." He brought his face closer to hers, his lips inches away from hers. The heat of her breath teased him and made him want her with a force so strong that he could barely think. His body was on fire with need for her. He'd never felt this way about a woman before in his life. He didn't know when she'd gotten under his skin like this.

"Jamal…"

Capturing her lips, he devoured her mouth, savoring the softness of her lips and the taste of her tongue. Jamal pulled her closer as if he was trying to melt with her. She didn't fight the heat. Her spicy response made him harder than concrete. But just like the end of a summer rain shower, she pushed him away.

"We can't do this." Her voice was a husky whisper. Could she get any sexier?

"Why not?"

"Because we're friends and this is just going to complicate everything." Rising to her feet, Michael smoothed her hands down her thighs. "I have to go."

"Don't go," he said as he closed the dark space between them. "My intentions were to show you the stars.

I don't want you to do anything that you're not ready for."

"I saw stars all right. Jamal, it's getting late and we have a meeting in the morning. I can't stargaze all night."

He stroked her arm. "That's fine. We're still going to eat the cake for breakfast, just in your office." Winking at her, Jamal walked over to the fire pit and doused the flames. "Next time we'll make the s'mores."

"You had s'mores?"

"Why else would I have a fire going in the summer?"

MJ smiled and stroked his cheek. "Aren't you just full of surprises, Mr. Carver. Next time, lead with the chocolate."

"Oh, so there will be a next time?"

She shook her head. "You're something else, but this was a good surprise and thank you for sharing the stars with me."

I'd share a lot more if you'd let me. Jamal took her hand in his and walked her to the driveway. "Call me and let me know you made it home safely," he said as he opened her car door.

"I will. And thank you again for dinner," MJ said as she closed the door. Watching her drive away, Jamal could only shake his head. He wanted this woman in his arms tonight, even if they kept all of their clothes on.

As Michael drove home, all she could think about was Jamal's kiss. That hot, soul-searing kiss had made her knees weak. Now her body ached with need. She needed Jamal's touch. Needed to feel him between her thighs.

Why did she kiss him? It wasn't their first kiss. She'd kissed him last year when they'd met at his house to talk about his situation with his mother and Brent's father. At that time, Jamal had been an emotional mess because Brent didn't know that his father was also Jamal's little brother's father. According to Jamal, Brent had unresolved anger issues with his father and he wondered how that would play into his relationship with the little boy after Brent Sr.'s death.

But that had been a gentle kiss. A friendly smooch that said, *I support you.* But this kiss… This kiss said, *I want you. I need you.* And boy, did she want him. It just wasn't going to be good for her heart.

He was a playboy. He'd even admitted that he hadn't wanted to settle down. Had something changed? Was he really trying to be with her as more than a friend or had they just gotten caught up in the heat of the moment?

As she pulled into her driveway, Michael sent Jamal a text. I made it home.

She wasn't sure if hearing his voice would make her turn around and live out her shower fantasy with him. Grabbing the cake slices, she exited the car and walked up to her front door. When her phone rang, shattering the silence around her, she nearly dropped her purse and the cake.

"Hello?"

"Your text was nice, but I could've sworn I asked you to call me."

"Jamal, go to bed."

"I will, at some point. Have you walked in the house yet?"

"Unlocking the door now."

"Good. And when you activate your security system, I'll let you go."

"You're all about protection, huh?" Michael keyed in her alarm code. "Done."

"Sleep well, beautiful. See you in the morning."

"Good night." Michael floated to her bedroom on the promise of seeing Jamal in the morning. She didn't even notice the text message she'd missed from Nic.

Jamal didn't sleep well, so when morning came it felt as if it was too soon. His body was so keyed up from wanting MJ that he would have to take a run, and a cold shower would certainly follow. Now he understood Lu-Lu's insanity from one kiss. Well, kind of. Lu-Lu was crazy, while he was just falling hard for the most amazing woman he'd ever met. Pulling himself out of bed, Jamal tugged on his running shorts, grabbed his sneakers and a bottle of water. Even though it was five after six, it was hot in Atlanta already. Jamal started with a slow jog and sped up as he started thinking about what Michael was doing this morning.

Did she sleep alone last night? Did he cross her mind? Was she going to act as if nothing had happened between them when he walked into her office in a few hours? He slowed his gait; he was going to see her in a few hours. Would he be able to handle that?

I got this, he thought as he started running again. Mile one was easy. Mile two, he ran into Lucy.

"Good morning, handsome," she said, seeming to appear from nowhere.

"Morning."

"Isn't this a beautiful green space? I love running here. I wish I'd known that you were working out this morning."

Jamal stopped and gave her a sidelong glance. "Yeah. Lucy, enjoy your run." He tore off as if he was Usain Bolt. Once he'd run for three miles, Jamal was tired. Glancing at his watch, he saw that it was time to head home so that he could get ready to meet MJ.

As he ran home, Jamal glanced over his shoulder to make sure Lucy hadn't followed him. He smiled when he made it home without encountering her again. Now he could focus his attention on MJ. And he hoped that she'd brought the chocolate cake in for them to enjoy over coffee. That cold shower was going to work miracles for him after his morning run.

Michael wanted to call in sick, but since she was the boss, that couldn't happen. Besides, she was the one who'd invited Jamal and his company to work on the biggest account in her company's history.

"What was I thinking?" she muttered as she rose from her bed and headed to the shower. She'd missed two calls from Mimi and she didn't care because she was in no position to run this morning. All night, Michael had dreamed of Jamal taking his kiss deeper and making all of her fantasies come true. But when she woke up holding her pillow and not Jamal, she had to get her act together.

Business. Focus on business.

Michael took the coldest shower that she could stand.

Her mind had conjured up erotic visions of Jamal last night, of his magical tongue touching her most sensitive spots. But in the light of day, she realized that she had to sit across from him and talk real business. She had to listen to him plan how to keep this jazz fest safe.

Get your hormones under control, girl, she thought as she stepped underneath the cold spray. *It was just one amazing kiss. Not as if it was your first amazing kiss.*

But it was. Michael let the cold water wash over her shoulders. She'd never been kissed like that before, and if she was honest, she knew she wanted more. Needed more. Jamal had awakened a passion inside her that she'd never felt before. He was everything she wanted and that scared her because she had a nagging fear that she might not be enough for him.

God, help me, she thought as she shut the water off.

Chapter 5

Michael walked into her office with a smile on her face and the bag containing the cake slices. Not the most nutritious breakfast, but she didn't mind sharing an unhealthy heap of goodness with Jamal.

"Good morning, Ms. Jane. Your nine o'clock is here."

"He's early." Michael looked at her watch and then glanced at the waiting area. "Nic? What are you doing here?"

Nic rose to his feet, smiling as he walked over to her. "I sent you a text last night, but I guess you were busy." He nodded toward the Sunshine Café bag in her hand. "Is that place any good?"

"I don't have time for this, Nic. I have… You know what? Let's kill two birds with one stone. I'm meeting with the head of a security company and you guys will have to meet eventually, so let's do it now."

"Great. What company are you thinking of using?"

"First Line of Defense. Let's go into my office." She expelled a frustrated sigh as they walked down the narrow hallway.

"MJ, I'm sorry about yesterday. I had no right to assume I could monopolize your private time. I miss our brainstorming sessions, you know."

Facing him with her hand on her office door, Michael sighed. "Nic, once upon a time, I thought we were going to be together. So, those brainstorming sessions and telling you all of my dreams and plans when you let me get a word in edgewise really meant something more than business to me. At the end of the day, I wasted a lot of time auditioning to be your woman and I didn't get the part. And since I didn't get the part, I will no longer be playing the role."

"Don't be like that. Bitter doesn't look good on you."

Michael raised her right eyebrow then smiled. "Bitter? Hardly. Babe, I'm better and I prove that every time I look at you and don't punch you in your face." She opened the door and walked in the office.

Nic followed and sat across from her desk. "I have reached out to some local artists and they're super excited about the jazz fest. So, I wanted to bring over some of their music for you to listen to. Then we could come up with a marketing plan to attract their listeners and let people who don't know about them discover them at the jazz fest."

"That's an interesting idea. I was thinking that we

do a jazz sampler CD and put them around different hot spots in the city. And we should expand the number of venues that we use."

"As long as my club gets top billing, I don't mind."

Michael leaned back in her chair. "About that… You can't be so self-serving, Nic. The reason why the New Orleans festivals work so well is that all of the clubs and venues come together to make it successful. There are about fifteen other clubs in the Atlanta area that could bring in more people, more artists, and from a marketing standpoint, this would put you in front of people who don't know about your club."

"That's what I'm talking about. What clubs are you thinking about bringing on board?"

Michael pulled out her tablet and handed it to him. "Here's the list of clubs."

As Nic read over the list, Michael's receptionist announced that Jamal was there to see her.

"Give me just a minute and I'll be out to meet him." Turning to Nic, she asked, "What do you think about the list?"

"There are two clubs here that I don't want to be involved with."

"Don't tell me there is beef in the jazz community."

"Vonnie Love is not someone I trust," he said, pointing to the Love Jazz listing. "He…"

"Used to be your partner. I know. I thought you guys had straightened everything out?"

Nic grimaced. "Not working with Love or Lucy Becker."

Michael rose to her feet and smoothed her pencil skirt. "I'll be right back and we can discuss this later."

Jamal looked around the waiting area and was impressed by MJ's style. Earth tones, abstract art on the walls. This was the kind of setting that made you not hate waiting. Calming, for someone else. Right now, he wanted to see her. They'd get to business, but he had to kiss her again.

And there she was, looking sexier than a woman should look this time of morning. That green skirt hugged those curves like he wanted to and the white ruffled shirt made her look like a present for him to unwrap.

"Good morning, beautiful." Jamal crossed over to her and drew Michael into his arms.

"Hi, Jamal." She took a step back. "Sorry to keep you waiting."

"Not a problem."

"Nic, the guy who's putting the jazz fest together, is here, and since you're going to do security for the festival, I thought you two should meet and talk about your plans."

"Oh, I'm hired like that?"

Michael smiled. "Yes. If you want the job it's yours."

"Is today the day I get everything I want? Because..."

"Down, boy." She pressed her hand against his chest. "We'll see how you hold up after the burpees."

Not willing to wait another second to feel her lips, Jamal leaned in and kissed her deep and slow. His hands roamed her back as she seemed to melt against him. All he wanted to do was lift her in his arms and bury himself inside her sweetness until she sang out in pleasure.

Business. I'm here for a business meeting. Jamal pulled back. "Sorry about that. But…"

"We'd better stop this. Nic is waiting inside." She wiped the lipstick from his lips.

"You still got my cake, right? I skipped breakfast for that."

"The cake is still waiting. Let's go."

Jamal was happy to walk behind Michael if for no other reason than to admire that skirt and silently thank the designer who made it.

Once they walked in the office, Nic and Jamal locked eyes. "Gentlemen," Michael began. "Jamal, meet Nicolas Prince. Nic, meet Jamal Carver, owner of First Line of Defense."

They shook hands then sat down. "First Line of Defense, huh? Were you a football player or something?"

"No, I'm a marine, so I know about defending and protecting real people." Jamal decided that he didn't like this Nic fellow.

"Excuse me."

Michael intervened. "Now, let's talk about what we're going to need to keep this event safe."

Jamal reached into his jacket pocket and pulled out his tablet. "Here's my plan for venue safety. There will be a guard posted at the entrance and at all doors. You're going to be looking at more people than you would normally have at any of these venues. Metal detectors are a good idea as well."

"Metal detectors, Jamal?" Michael questioned. "It's not that kind of crowd."

"I'm with Michael on this. For one, metal detectors

will cost us money. Plus, they turn people off and remind them of why they hate airports."

"Show of hands—how many people in this room run a security firm?" Jamal raised his hand. "Safety matters, and if you want to ensure safety and keep your insurance costs down, you need metal detectors. Nothing is going to sink your event like a riot or crowd injury."

Michael nodded. "Good point."

"Well, I still don't like the idea. Why not a pat down? Metal detectors are going to slow the lines down."

"And keep people alive," Jamal interjected. "You handle the music and the booze and leave the security to me." He winked at Michael then moved on to the next plan for the outdoor part of the security detail, which included working with the Atlanta Police Department for crowd control and patrols around the venues.

"This is very impressive," Michael said. "But then again, I wouldn't expect anything less from you, Jamal."

Nic shot them questioning glances but didn't say anything for a beat. "I've seen you in my club."

"Yes, you have. It's a great place." *But you better believe you won't see me there again.*

"Thanks. I try to keep it upscale. And it's one of the best places to meet women, but you already know that."

Jamal clenched his teeth then glanced at Michael. Her expression was unreadable.

"Guys, can we focus on the jazz festival? Jamal, can you get me a copy of the security plan? Nic, I think we need to get you on some local shows and featured in some entertainment magazines to build a buzz. Once we get the partnerships with the other jazz clubs nailed down, we will see if we can get a segment on *Good Day Atlanta*. And you need to play nice with Mimi because I want her to feature this on her blog."

"Oh, Lord."

"She has millions of followers."

"Yeah, Mimi's minions." Nic rolled his eyes. "Isn't she in New Orleans now?"

"New Orleans and Atlanta," Jamal said.

"You follow her blog?" Nic asked incredulously.

"She's married to my best friend." *Clown.*

"Oh, yeah. I forgot Firecracker got married. God bless him."

"Nic!"

He threw his hands up. "Just kidding. Well, it seems as if we're going in the right direction here. Thank you for the meeting, Michael. Let's do this again next week." Nic glanced over at Jamal. "Michael, may I have a word with you in private?"

Jamal shook his head and smirked. "I'll wait for you outside."

"No, wait here," she said. "Nic, I'll walk you outside."

Alone in Michael's office, Jamal walked over to the window and looked out over the city. Nic was acting like a jealous ex. He couldn't help but wonder if he was the reason MJ was skeptical about getting serious with him.

"What did she ever see in that self-righteous prick?"

"Is that the guy who took a trip between your thighs last night?"

"Really? This is what you wanted to talk about?"

Nic placed his hand on her shoulder. "That guy is a player, and if you're trying to..."

Michael snatched away from him. "I'm going to stop you right here. My personal life is none of your concern. I don't need your advice, your opinion or thoughts on what I should do or who I should do it with."

"I know we didn't end up the way you wanted us to, but I was always honest with you."

"Nicolas, whatever we had is officially history. And for the record, Jamal and I are friends, not that it is any of your business."

"I miss you being my friend, Michael."

"We were never friends. And if the way you just behaved in that meeting is how you do friendship, I'm not interested. After this event, we're done, Nic. Business and personal."

He gave her a sidelong glance. "Well, if that's how you want it."

"That's how it's going to be. And if I were you, I'd send Mimi an orchid. She loves those flowers."

"Yeah, I'll take it under advisement."

Michael pressed the elevator button. "Goodbye, Nic." She didn't even wait for the door to close before heading back to her office. Internally, though, she was muddled with emotions. It wasn't as if she didn't know that Jamal was a man about town. But somehow, hearing it come out of Nic's mouth made her feel as if she was being foolish to think that there could be something between them more than sizzling kisses. Did everybody know he was a player? Was he okay with that?

"Jamal and I are just friends," she muttered as she walked back to her office. "Nice view, huh?"

Jamal turned around. "I think this is a better one."

"Ready for that cake?"

He nodded and crossed over to her. "Tell me something. Did you and Nic date?"

"Something like that, but it was a long time ago."

"Left you scarred, though?"

Michael speared him with an icy glance. "Jamal, I don't want to talk about it. We can eat cake or you can leave."

"Ouch."

She arched her eyebrow at him as if she was waiting for his decision. "I'm always going to choose cake," he said then gave her backside a soft smack. "But let me say this—we're not all alike."

"I know that. And I don't think you go to Nic's club trolling for women, either." Michael pulled the cake out of her desk drawer.

"There's something I've always wanted to ask you."

Michael handed Jamal his hunk of cake and a plastic fork. "I might answer."

"How did you end up with the name 'Michael'?"

She broke out laughing as she unwrapped her cake. "You know I must like you because I'm going to tell you the truth."

"The truth?"

"My marketing response to this question is that my parents thought I was going to be a boy and pre-wrote the birth certificate. But the truth is, my mother was a horrible speller. She wanted to name me Michelle. She couldn't spell it and I ended up Michael."

Jamal covered his grin with his hand. And Michael shook her head. "Go on and laugh," she said then took a bite of her cake. "You and Mimi are the only two people who know the truth."

"I'm willing to bet that your name has opened many doors."

"Yeah, well, it was hell getting into Spelman."

"What are your plans for tonight?" Jamal placed his hand on top of hers and peered into her eyes.

"You got another group of stars to show me?"

"No. I want to show you the moon and Venus."

Michael slipped her hand from underneath his and laughed. "You really are a nerd."

"Only you and my gran know this. When I was growing up, my mom had some issues. For most of my childhood, she was in and out of my life. It wasn't until I was ten that she was diagnosed with bipolar disorder. Once she got the right medication, everything was fine. But until she got better, it was Gran who took care of me. She showed me the universe and it started my fascination with the stars."

"How is your mom doing?"

"She and Daveon are doing well. They actually moved down to Savannah. I think Brent Sr.'s death hit Mom harder than she wanted to admit."

"How does Brent feel about all of this?"

"He and Daveon are getting closer and that's the important thing."

Michael nodded in agreement as she munched on her cake. "So, taking me to Venus tonight?"

"Yes. And this is a rare trip, Ms. Jane."

"Is that so?" She placed her fork on the side of her box. "Now, is this going to be after our little gym thing? I'm sorry I missed our scheduled time this morning, but I wasn't feeling it."

What she didn't say was how his kiss had kept her up all night with erotic dreams that made her think about calling him for a booty call.

"You want to lose, huh?" Jamal leaned back in his chair. "You're trying to set me up with this cake, but it is not going to work."

"We'll see, cake man. All of yours is gone and I still have half of mine to eat as I celebrate my victory."

Jamal was about to say something when his cell phone rang. "I have to take this. I'll see you at the gym around six, right?"

"Sounds good." As Michael watched him walk out the door, she wondered if the call he had to take was from another woman. Standing up and looking out the window, Michael decided she wasn't going to drive herself crazy. Jamal was her friend, they were having fun and she couldn't expect him not to see other people.

"I'm worse than Mimi," she muttered.

Chapter 6

"Brent, slow down. Did you say my company is named in this lawsuit?" Jamal slammed into his car.

"I got a copy of it about an hour ago. Listen, we can beat this. I just need to know what kind of security plan you had and if the promoter made any changes."

"Nothing on paper, but from what the guys were saying, the shooting happened outside and we weren't hired to protect the parking lot. However, I expected my guys to make sure no guns got on the property. The sheriff's department should've handled that. Shit, I don't need this right now."

"I know. But we need to get in front of this right now and get the promoter to take the heat."

Jamal muttered a string of curse words. "I'm on my

way." He sped to his buddy's office and hoped that the story of this lawsuit wouldn't make the news.

When Jamal arrived at Brent's office, his good mood from talking with Michael had worn off. Part of him could hear Nic telling her that he wouldn't work with First Line of Defense because of this lawsuit.

Brent met Jamal in the lobby. "You look like hell and we haven't even gone over the suit yet."

"I was thinking about the projects that I'm probably going to lose because of this suit, including the jazz fest."

"You and Michael working on that together?"

"Was with her when you called. Met that dude Nic and I can see him talking a lot of shit."

"Let's take this in my office," Brent said then pointed to his assistant. "Can we get some coffee? And hold my calls, unless it's Mimi."

"Yes, sir," she said.

Any other time, Jamal would've made a joke about Brent being whipped. He was definitely going to keep this under his hat for now. Brent sat down and pulled out the paperwork.

"Here's what we're going to do. We're calling the promoter. The Wright family seemed as if they wanted to blame the entire world for their son's death. It's understandable, but ridiculous. Your company, the Fulton County Sheriff's Office and the promoter are named in the lawsuit."

"And how is that going to get me off the hook on this lawsuit?"

"Let me do my thing," he said as he dialed the number. "This is Brent Daniels. I need to speak with Roger Kelly. I'll hold."

Jamal shook his head as Brent scowled at the phone. When Jamal's cell phone chimed in his pocket, he gritted his teeth because it was a Google alert. He didn't even have to look at it to know the lawsuit had gone public. This was going to be a cluster.

"Yes, I received the lawsuit against you and that's why I'm calling. First Line of Defense is my client and you didn't hire them to provide security in the parking lot. I'm looking at that now. Can I represent you? As soon as you get out front and say my current client had nothing to do with the shooting that happened at your event, I'll take it under consideration." Brent hung up the phone and shot his friend an I-told-you-so look. "Crisis controlled."

"Yeah, but the news is already out there." Jamal held his phone out to Brent. "The blogs are talking as well as the local papers."

"Well, I can't do anything about that until the promoter issues a statement."

When Jamal's phone rang, he knew he had to get to his office and try to put part of this fire out. Brent shot him a stern look.

"Jamal, don't talk to the media."

"Hopefully, they aren't camped out outside my office. Leslie is calling. And my receptionist never calls me." Jamal stood up and shook Brent's hand. "Thanks for helping me with this."

"Thank me later when you get the bill."

"Whatever."

* * *

Michael picked up her phone then put it down again. She looked at the news alert for the third time. *He has to be so upset.* Rising to her feet, she paced the length of her office. She felt horrible for Jamal and like a jerk for thinking that he'd run out to talk to another woman. He'd probably gotten a call about the lawsuit and gone to see his lawyer. Walking over to her desk, Michael grabbed her purse. She needed some air. As soon as she got to the parking lot, Michael saw Mimi coming her way.

"What's up, lady? I was coming to see if you and Jamal were huddled together about this lawsuit."

"No. I was just going to take a drive and… Mimi, I'm a jerk."

Mimi raised her eyebrow at her friend. "Now, why would you say that?"

"Jamal was here earlier. He's going to do security for the jazz fest. And Nic was here."

"Oh. My. God! What did old, stupid and thoughtless do?"

Michael dropped her head for a moment. "Got inside my head. He was like, *oh, Jamal, I see you leaving my club with a bunch of women*. Then when I walked him out, he was all *I hope you're not serious about him. He's a player.* So, I'm sitting here feeling like boo-boo the fool and Jamal got a phone call and left suddenly. All I could think was he must be going to meet with some other woman."

"Wait. Why do you care what your friend does and

who he does it with?" Mimi laughed. "Somebody is catching feelings."

"This is why I can't talk to you sometimes," MJ groaned. "I don't know what I was more upset about—Nic calling himself looking out for me or actually falling for Jamal's sexy nerd act last night."

"Sexy nerd? Okay, I need details," Mimi exclaimed.

"Nothing to tell. He cooked dinner and we stargazed." Because she didn't want to hear Mimi go on and on about her hiding her feelings, MJ left out the part about the kiss.

"Are you serious?"

"It was actually endearing," MJ replied.

"I bet it was. And I hope you told Nic where he could stick his unsolicited advice. That asshole."

"You're missing the bigger point, Mimi. That call was about this news alert and his company. How am I going to get serious with him when I have all of these doubts?"

"First, you have to stop driving yourself crazy. Secondly, if you want him, go get him."

"Jamal is happy being single, and I'm…"

"You don't know if he's happy or not because you haven't talked to him about how he feels. You just assume. I told you that you should've been honest with him a long time away."

"And I would take advice from the woman who ran to New Orleans when she realized that she was in love because…?"

"Funny. Real funny, MJ. My point is, learn from my

mistakes. Don't head to another city or state when what you want is staring you right in your face."

But what if he wants something entirely different? Not looking to get my heart broken again, Mimi.

"I know that look, MJ. And your heart wouldn't have been broken in the first place if Nic wasn't a jerk who was more concerned about what you could do for him than how you felt about him. Despite my first impression of Jamal, the one thing he's not is a big jerk."

Michael smiled. "I know."

Mimi furrowed her brows. "Okay. So, you know when a guy opens up to you the way Jamal did, it's not just because he wants to only get into your pants."

"I can't. I'm not ready to get my heart stomped on again."

"And you know this is going to happen because you can see into the future now? Girl, give me those Powerball numbers."

"Shut up." She sighed in exasperation at her friend. "What's wrong with being a little cautious?"

"Nothing, but you're not being cautious. You're being ridiculous. How about you stop acting as if you can read that man's mind? Talk to him, please. Or I'm writing about this on my blog."

"And I will drop you in Lake Lanier."

Mimi grinned and folded her arms across her chest. "Whatever. Let's go find him."

"How about I do it on my own and you go sit on your husband's lap."

"Good idea, and when you find Jamal, tell him how you feel. Because this has moved way beyond a rebound thing and I'm glad. MJ, you deserve to be happy, and from what I see, Jamal makes you happy."

Michael had known for the longest time that Jamal was far from a rebound fling. She hoped that he was the real thing, but how could she be sure when she'd been so wrong about Nic? Granted, she was over Nic, but she couldn't forget the moment she knew she'd made a fool of herself. She'd poured her heart out to Nic, only to hear him tell her that she was a great friend, but he couldn't see himself settling down with her.

Broken and hurt beyond words, Michael had vowed to never allow another man to make her feel so small. Not when she'd worked so hard to be the perfect half to a successful man. She hadn't wanted to be like her mother, always feeling subservient to a man. Michael's father had been a teacher at the local high school and her mother hadn't earned a high school diploma. He'd lorded that over her for years.

Michael knew she would never be with a man who treated her that way. She'd thought that she and Nic were equals and he'd see that together they'd be an un-stoppable force. But that night, she understood how her mother had felt all those years. She felt the pain of being treated as if she wasn't good enough.

If she could do it over, she'd be a better daughter to her mom and not always take her father's side.

Now here she was in that same spot—again. Because expecting Jamal Carver to settle down just seemed stupid. Still, she headed to his office and hoped to find him alone so that they could have the conversation that she'd been dreading.

Mimi was right about one thing, though. Jamal did make her happy. Would telling him how she felt change all of that?

Jamal had entered his office from the back entrance and was avoiding all phone calls. He had been trying to take Brent's advice. But all of the reporters outside of his office made him want to say something to clear his name. He'd fired the men who'd dropped the ball on the security inside the event. But it wasn't his fault that the sheriff hadn't provided adequate security outside of the concert.

This lawsuit could bankrupt him or make it difficult for First Line of Defense to gain new clients. "Shit," he muttered as he grabbed a bottle of whiskey from his desk drawer. Jamal started to ignore the ringing of his cell phone, but he saw Michael's picture flash across the screen. Then he answered. "Hey."

"Where are you?"

"At my office."

"I'm on my way over there. Jamal, I think I can help you deal with the media."

"That would be awesome. Come in the back entrance. I'll be waiting for you."

"See you in about twenty minutes." Michael hoped she didn't run into a traffic jam. Her prayers were answered and she arrived at Jamal's office fifteen minutes after they'd hung up. She wasn't surprised to see that a number of media folks were roaming around the parking lot. "News travels way too fast these days." She parked in the back like Jamal had suggested and saw him sitting on the top of his Mustang's trunk.

"Hi."

Jamal hopped off the car and crossed over to MJ. She wrapped her arms around him, thinking that her hug would comfort him. But the heat from his body simply drove her crazy. Inhaling, she filled her soul with his masculine scent. Pulling back, she stroked his cheek. "You okay?"

"As okay as one can be in a media circus." Jamal held her around the waist.

"Maybe I can help you with this."

"No. Our relationship is becoming too business-oriented."

"But, Jamal, this is what I do. And friends help each other in times of need, right?"

Smirking, he shook his head. "Friends, huh? Ever think about what things would be like between us if we were more than friends?"

Michael blinked, wondering if she'd been broadcasting her emotions or if Jamal really wanted to move beyond no-strings. "Do you really think you and I should be focusing on that right now?"

"Today. Tomorrow. Next week. It doesn't matter. Just answer the question."

"Jamal, I—I…" Before Michael could utter another word, flashbulbs went off in their faces. Then the questions.

"Mr. Carver, what are your thoughts on the lawsuit?"

"Were your guards negligent in protecting the parking lot?"

"How did the gun get into the venue?"

Jamal dropped his hands from Michael's waist and turned toward the door of the office, moving to usher her inside. Michael's instincts took over. "Mr. Carver will release a statement in a few days, but right now is not the time to talk about a suit that my client hasn't had a chance to review with his attorney. At this time we offer our condolences to the family."

When the media backed away, she looked up at Jamal, who was giving her a slow handclap as they headed inside.

"I see you're really awesome at what you do. You just came up with that off the top of your head?"

"Yep. It's classic crisis-control verbiage. We're all sorry when someone dies, and while I'm sure you and Brent have looked over the lawsuit, I don't know what you've discussed."

"I might need to take you up on that offer."

Michael raised her right eyebrow. "I can't believe you thought you could do this without me."

"Now I'm forever in your debt. I'll do anything you want to pay it off." Jamal pulled Michael against his chest. She melted in his arms, and as much as she wanted to open her mouth and spill all of her feelings to him, she couldn't. Wouldn't. Didn't. Their lips touched, and in one swift motion, they were locked in a hot kiss. Michael wasn't even sure how it happened—whether she kissed him or not. But when their tongues touched, it didn't matter. She felt as if she was going to pass out as he deepened the kiss; her thighs trembled when he sucked her tongue, making her mouth feel as if it was made of honey. And when he nibbled her bottom lip, her panties were soaked with desire. What kind of magical lips did this man have?

Placing her hand on his chest, Michael pulled away from him, breathless. "Well, that's one way to work off your debt."

"Then I'm going to have to get in trouble more often to create more debt."

"Please don't." She released a deep sigh. "I don't know if I can handle those payments."

"That's just the beginning." Jamal kissed her on the forehead. "So, let's get this statement together."

"I can have it written and ready for you to hand out before you take me to lunch." She winked at him and followed him down the hallway to his office.

When Michael sat at his desk, she seemed as if she belonged there. "Once we're done, we can email the document to Brent to make sure he's all right with everything I say."

"Which is going to be?"

MJ typed without saying a word and then she turned the screen around to Jamal. "Everything I said to those reporters outside."

"Cool. Yeah, send that to Brent because he told me not to talk to the media." When his cell phone rang, Jamal wasn't surprised to see that it was his lawyer. "What's up, Brent?"

"I see you have MJ handling the media. Smart move. The promoter just released a statement about your involvement in the security for the club."

"Saying what?"

"That what happened in the parking lot had nothing to do with First Line of Defense and now this family is trying to sue everyone associated with the concert. We're backing away from this like we have skates on."

"Good. Maybe these reporters are gone now," Jamal said as he walked toward the lobby. He was happy to see the parking lot was empty. "I'm no longer a hot topic."

"That's a good thing. I'm going to let you get back to MJ, because my lunch—I mean, my wife—just walked in."

"Whipped."

"You want to be. Take a page out of my book and go after that woman. I'm about to get mine. Later."

Jamal shook his head when he shoved his phone in his pocket. He never thought that he'd be jealous of a married man. But he wanted that now. Jamal knew from the moment he kissed Michael that he didn't want every woman in Atlanta. He needed MJ to be his one-and-only.

Now, how was he going to convince her of that? Jamal returned to his office, and while he stood in the doorway, he watched Michael sending a text. How could she be so sexy doing something so simple? He wanted to take her crossed legs and wrap them around his waist as he dived deep into her sweet wetness. He wanted to hear her moan his name as she came. Wanted to feel her nails scratch his back as he made her come again and again.

"Jamal?"

"Yes?"

"Did you hear anything I said?"

"Yeah, yeah. Lunch, right?"

MJ stood up and crossed over to him. "No, silly." She tapped his cheek. "I said I can't make lunch because I have another fire to put out. But I'm looking forward to seeing Venus tonight."

He grabbed her hand and kissed it. "I'll see you at the gym first, though."

"We're going to have to reschedule your beatdown. See you tonight." Watching MJ walk out the door made him harder than a man should get watching a fully dressed woman walk away from him. She had a shape like the iconic soft-drink bottle and all he wanted to do was peel those clothes off her and spread her across his desk and make love to her.

"Damn it, I got to make her mine," he muttered as he crossed over to his desk.

Chapter 7

Michael sat at her desk and groaned. Three hours. Three hours of whining and complaining. She was going to drop Cleo Parker as a client as soon as the check cleared. Marketing an author shouldn't be this hard, but if Cleo was going to argue with every reader who didn't like her sci-fi romance novels, she couldn't expect that she was going to make any bestseller list.

When that woman walked out of her office, Michael stood up and did a happy dance. Glancing at her watch, she realized that she wasn't going to make her spin class before going to see Jamal. *Maybe I should just let him work out my thighs. Stop it! This is how it all falls apart, adding sex to the mix. But God knows I want this man.*

Grabbing her purse, she tried to get her hormones

under control before heading to Jamal's. *Cold shower on deck.*

When Michael arrived at her place, she was shocked to see Nic parked on the curb. She parked her car and said a silent prayer before getting out and walking over to Nic.

"What's up?" she asked when he got out of the car.

"I'm sure you've seen the news about your boy's lawsuit."

"And I'm sure you've seen the update about him not being responsible for the shooting. This could've been handled with a phone call—better yet, a text."

"I'm worried about you. I know how women get when they see their friends fall into a happily-ever-after. Don't think that you have to settle for a man like Jamal."

"A man like Jamal?"

"Yes."

"And do you have a better suggestion for my life, since I'm obviously under some kind of undue influence and can't make decisions for myself."

Nic wiped his hand across his face. "That's not what I'm saying, but just because Mimi got married, it doesn't mean that her husband's best friend is the one for you."

"Was I unclear earlier when I told you that my personal life is *not* your concern?"

"Even if you don't consider me your friend, I still care about you, MJ. I want you to be happy, and if I'm not the guy to…"

"Go home, Nic. Go home and don't ever say these words to me ever again. You don't have the right to offer me advice about my love life when you held it hostage for years because you love yourself more than you can ever love me or anyone else." She fought the urge to slap the taste out of his mouth. The mouth that she once craved and dreamed of kissing for the rest of her life. Shaking her head, she realized that after kissing Jamal, she'd learned that she would've shortchanged herself for life if she'd stayed on with Nic.

"When your heart gets broken, don't say I didn't warn you."

Michael walked away because she wasn't sure how long she'd be able to keep her hands to herself.

Jamal decided that tonight, he'd bring MJ inside for dinner. He made lemon pepper chicken and linguine. Then to add some veggies to the mix, he prepared a green salad with spicy vinaigrette dressing on the side. Gran would be proud.

Jamal just hoped that his dessert would be MJ, naked. After they saw Venus, of course, because he didn't want her to know he'd brought her there just to seduce her. But that was his endgame.

However, this wasn't typical playboy Jamal seduction. He wanted to brand her as his tonight. Wanted to make her realize that he was hers for the taking and all she needed to do was open her arms.

Walking into his sunroom, he lit two candles and then opened the blackout blinds so the last rays of the sun could filter into the room. When the moon rose and the stars came out, this was going to be the most amazing backdrop for dinner. Pulling out two big pillows, he set up the table for intimacy. How much longer did he have to wait for her to show up, though? When the doorbell rang, Jamal rushed to the door hoping to see MJ's smiling face on the other side. But when he opened the door and saw Lucy on his doorstep, he wanted to disappear. *I should've never brought her here to wait for Triple A that night*, he thought, remembering the one time he wished he hadn't been such a gentleman.

Jamal swung the door open and leaned against the doorjamb. "What are you doing here?"

"Oh, Jamal, I saw the news about the shooting and the lawsuit. Are you all right?"

"Yeah, I'm good, but I'm a little busy right now."

Lucy stood on her tiptoes in an attempt to look over Jamal's shoulder. "I guess you have someone in here comforting you already, huh? So typical."

"Lu-Lucy, I've had enough of your quasi-stalking. We went out once. One date. I never made any kind of promises to you for you to be acting like this."

"Jamal, I know we have a connection. Just give us a chance." She took a step closer to him.

"Leave or I'm going to call the police."

"One day, you're going to be so sorry about how you treat women. Someone is going to make you pay!" Lucy stomped off the porch and slammed into her car. Jamal could only shake his head as she sped down the road.

Michael wiped the bright red lipstick from her lips and glanced at herself in the mirror. Why did she feel like she was getting ready for the prom? This wasn't her first date with Jamal, but something about tonight felt different.

She reapplied her lipstick and adjusted her strapless sundress. Maybe tonight she would follow Mimi's advice and tell him how she felt. Maybe.

On the ride over to Jamal's, she forced herself not to allow Nic's asinine comments get under her skin. People could change, and who was to say that Jamal hadn't? They'd been hanging out together quite frequently, and other than the incident at the restaurant, there were no signs of him seeing other people.

"You shouldn't have to be a private investigator to date," she muttered as she turned into Jamal's neighborhood. She didn't notice the car parked across the street taking pictures of her as she emerged from the car.

Jamal opened the door before Michael could ring the bell. "Don't you look amazing," he said.

Michael's mouth hung open as she drank in Jamal's physique in black linen pants and a formfitting white T-shirt that hugged his rippling muscles. His ebony brown skin was smooth and reminded her of the finest chocolate. Her mouth watered as she thought about running her tongue across his chest. "As do you." Her voice was husky with yearning. She didn't care about seeing Venus; she wanted to see what was underneath those clothes. Feel his body pressed against hers as they kissed again.

"Come on in. Dinner is waiting in the sunroom."

She followed him inside and was very impressed by the open space of the sunroom. The flickering candles and glowing night sky were breathtaking. "No telescope tonight?"

"Not yet. This room is one of the main reasons I

bought this house. In the winter, I come in here and watch the sky sparkle."

"You're really a nerd."

He kissed her on the cheek then helped her down onto one of the oversize pillows. "I'm only going to take a few more nerd comments."

"What are you going to do, nerd?"

"Take your food away." Jamal reached for her plate and she grabbed his wrist.

"That's just cruel."

He leaned into her, pressing his nose against her. "Do you know how delicious your lips look right now? I'm thinking about cherry pie."

Before she could reply, Jamal captured her lips in a hot kiss—nibbling and sucking on her full bottom lip until she shivered. Pulling back, Jamal smiled at her then licked his lips. "You taste even better than you look."

"Jamal, if you keep kissing me like that, we're not going to make it through dinner."

Lowering his head, he brushed his lips across hers. "Promise?"

"I'm hungry and this food smells so good. Can we eat?"

Jamal bit his bottom lip. "I know what I'd like to eat, but I won't be selfish right now." He took his seat beside her and they dug into their meals. Michael was once again impressed by Jamal's culinary skills.

"If you ever want a third career, I think I see chef in your future." Michael struggled not to slurp her noodles. "Why do we even go out to eat?"

"Because I hate washing dishes. But, if you promise to wear that red lipstick more often, I will cook for you every night."

"Wow, you're easy."

"I'm choosing to take that as a compliment." Jamal rose to his feet. "I forgot the drinks. Sweet tea work for you?"

"Come on, now. Who doesn't want sweet tea?"

As Jamal walked out of the room, Michael gazed out of the windows, amazed by the view of the night sky. Being surrounded by all of the natural beauty, she felt comfortable and ready to open up to Jamal. Tonight was as good a night as any to tell him how she felt about him.

"Here we go." He handed her a glass of tea as she turned around. "Beautiful, isn't it?"

"It is. Makes me wish I could paint. This would be a great painting."

Jamal set his glass down and pulled Michael into his arms. "Look," he said as he pointed to a group of stars. "The Big Dipper. Actually, it's not a constellation, but only the most visible part of Ursa Major, which is the constellation The Big Bear. And don't you dare say it."

"I'm not, because it's just stating the obvious." MJ gave him a quick kiss on the cheek. "Looking at the sky is getting interesting because of you."

Jamal stroked her hair and snuggled closer to her. "MJ." His lips were so close to her ear, she could feel his words. "There are a lot of things that have gotten interesting because of you."

"What are we doing? Jamal, I know you're… I can't pretend we're just friends anymore."

"Good, because I'm tired of doing that myself."

"Can we be honest for a second? I don't want to be hurt and I don't want you to feel like…"

"MJ, I'd never hurt you. And since we're being honest, I've never felt this way about a woman before."

"Jamal."

He stroked her cheek before devouring her lips. His kiss stirred her soul, made her desire drip between her thighs like a summer rain. He slipped his hands underneath her dress and between her thighs. Michael moaned as his thumbs brushed against her wetness. Her panties were soaked and a wet annoyance. She almost wanted to snatch them off, but Jamal made quick work of removing them. As quickly as he tossed them aside, Jamal dived between her thighs and lapped her sweetness. Michael tossed her head back, moaning in delight as his tongue danced around her clit, crying out his name as he stroked her thighs. She grabbed the back of his head, pushing him deeper inside.

When Michael came, it felt like an explosion from her soul. "Oh, Jamal!" Her body went limp and he drew her into his arms.

"You're officially my favorite dessert." He kissed her shoulder. "And that friend question is answered. We're no longer just friends. MJ, tonight I'm making every inch of you mine." He slowly slid her dress below her breasts and unsnapped her bra. "You're so beautiful." Slowly, he licked and sucked her rock-hard nipples while sliding her dress all the way down. Every touch, every lick ignited a fire inside her. Jamal made her body move to his will.

Moving down to her navel, Jamal used his tongue to explore Michael's curves and silky skin.

"Need to get a condom," he moaned. "Because I have to be inside you."

Michael nodded, unable to speak because she wanted him so badly.

Jamal practically ran into the bathroom. He grabbed a condom and stripped out of his pants and T-shirt. Tonight he felt like he was going to be making love for the first time. He paused. He would be making love to MJ. This wasn't a hookup, a fling or something that wouldn't mean anything in the morning. He was going to make love to the woman he was falling in love with. The one woman he was never going to let out of his heart.

Walking into the sunroom, he looked at MJ lying on the pillows. The word *goddess* came to mind. "MJ," he said as he crossed over to her. "I know I keep saying it, but you are beautiful."

She propped herself up on her elbows and her eyes roamed his nearly naked body. "And you don't look half-bad yourself. Come here."

"Yes, baby?"

MJ reached for the waistband of his boxer briefs. Tugging them down, she reached for his hardness and Jamal shook with anticipation when he felt the heat of her breath against his tip. Stroke. Lick. Suck. Jamal's knees quaked. Her tongue was magical and the softness of her lips nearly took him to the brink.

"Michael, Michael, Michael!" He stroked her hair as

she licked him like he was a melting ice-cream cone. "Need to be inside you, baby."

She pulled back from him, ending his sensuous torture. "I need you inside me, now."

Jamal ripped the condom package open and slid the sheath in place. As he joined her on the pillows, he thought about seeing her belly filled with his child while she wore his wedding ring. The image made him go still for a beat. Never in his life had he ever thought about family and marriage with a naked woman lying in wait.

He wrapped her legs around his waist and drove into her wetness. They ground against each other, dancing an erotic tango. She felt like heaven. Felt better than anything he'd ever experienced as she matched him thrust for thrust.

Any fantasy he'd ever had about MJ didn't match up to the reality and he couldn't be happier. "Yes, yes," she cried as they rocked back and forth. She tightened her thighs around him and Jamal exploded.

"Damn, baby, damn!"

MJ licked the side of his neck as she reached her climax. "Oh, Jamal."

He wrapped his arms around her and decided that he never wanted to let her go. "I may never let you leave."

"I may not want to." Moments later, they were both asleep and sated.

About an hour later, the sound of smashing glass woke the couple. Jamal leaped to his feet and pulled on his boxer briefs. "What in the hell?"

"What's going on?"

Jamal dashed down the hall to find out while Michael covered herself with her dress. When he got to the front door, he saw one of his planters had fallen and broken the side window. *This is weird*, he thought then brushed it off as a stray animal roaming his property.

"Everything all right?" Michael called out.

"Yeah. Probably a deer looking to eat my plants. I'm going to the garage to get some plywood." Opening the door, Jamal looked around to see if Bambi or his cousins were still running through the yard. When he didn't see anything, he crossed over to the garage and grabbed some wood to patch the window for the night.

He didn't notice a car at the end of the street and the driver watching his every move.

Chapter 8

Michael looked up at the ink-black sky and smiled. It was nice to know she wasn't in a one-sided romance. Jamal made her feel as if they were going to have a great future and she could open her heart to him without getting hurt.

"Hey," Jamal said when he walked into the sunroom. "You good?"

"Yeah. What time is it?"

He looked at his watch. "Two thirty. Let's go upstairs and sleep in the bed."

She shook her head. "I like it down here. It's still beautiful." Michael pointed to the sky. "Can't wait to see what it looks like when the sun rises."

Jamal eased down on the pillows with Michael and

pulled her into his arms. "It won't compare to you at all."

She leaned against his chest, and they looked up at the stars until they drifted back to sleep.

MJ woke up with a start, wondering if last night had been another dream. But her naked body let her know she hadn't been dreaming at all. Making love to Jamal had been better than a dream. He was as tender as he was passionate. A lover who gave as well as he received.

Turning to her side, she wondered where he was. The scent of coffee gave her an indication. Stretching her arms above her head, she drank in the beauty of the golden sunlight pouring in through wide windows. The warmth of the sun reflected MJ's mood, and the cheerful scene was made even better when Jamal walked in the room holding two mugs of coffee.

"Good morning, beautiful." He held out one of the cups to her after she sat up.

MJ inhaled the aroma of the coffee and smiled. "Umm, Dancing Goat blend. Mimi strikes again."

"I knew about Dancing Goat before she used it to seduce my boy."

Michael laughed. "It worked."

Leaning in and kissing her on the shoulder, Jamal grinned. "Is it working now?"

"We'll see. What are you going to do about that window?"

"I'm going to call someone out to replace it later. You hungry?"

"Starving."

"Let's cook something," he said as he set his coffee cup on the table.

"All right." Michael pulled her dress on and followed a shirtless Jamal into the kitchen. "Breakfast is my favorite meal."

"Then maybe I should sit back and watch."

"Well, you've cooked dinner for me, so I will be happy to cook you my famous cheese omelets."

"And I have to have garlic toast to go along with it."

She thrust her hip into his. "I like the way you think." Michael was impressed by Jamal's gourmet kitchen, stainless-steel appliances, copper pots hanging over the stove and a spice rack on the back of the stove.

"I see you, Bobby Flay."

"I told you my gran said you need to know how to cook. Let me see what you're working with."

"Point me to the eggs and cheese." Michael grabbed a frying pan and placed it on the stove. Jamal showed her where all the ingredients were for what she needed then sat back and watched her cook.

When she finished the omelets and baked the toast, Jamal was impressed by the beauty's skills in the kitchen. "I think we're never going to have to eat out again." Jamal accepted the plate Michael set in front of him.

"Don't get used to this. We still have to go to the Sunshine Café because I can't bake."

"Me either."

Jamal dug into his food and it was delicious. "This is good. We should just open a restaurant. You handle breakfast and I'll do dinner."

"What about lunch?"

"That's when we do each other." Jamal winked at her as she walked over to the other side of the bar with her plate.

"You are so bad."

"And I'm really good at it."

"As much as I'd love to hear and feel more about your bad behavior, I have some meetings about the jazz fest in a couple of hours."

Jamal's jaw tightened. "With Nic?"

"You don't like him much, huh?"

Jamal stuffed a piece of toast in his mouth. "What's the deal with you two?"

"There is no deal. He's a client."

Jamal raised his eyebrow at her. "Really?"

Michael tilted her head at him. "I know you're not playing the jealous-of-your-past card. Are you really serious right now?"

"Wait—you're turning my question into an argument?"

"No, but the implication of…"

"Let me stop you right there. I have nothing to do with any of my exes, but you and Nic are always around each other. I just want to make sure I'm not going to be blindsided."

"I don't roll like that, Jamal. If I had a smidgen of feelings for another man, I wouldn't have been with you last night, or even hanging out with you these past few months. But don't be that guy. Don't be the guy who acts like no other man was interested in a woman until he looked at her."

"Ouch."

"Jamal, I'm not going to bite my tongue because you gave me an orgasm."

He clasped his hands together. "How did we go from having a wonderful breakfast to having our first argument?"

"This isn't an argument. I was just setting you straight."

"Excuse me. Come here. We have to make up now." Jamal opened his arms to her. Michael laughed as she fell into his embrace.

"Maybe I overreacted. Fatal flaw of mine."

"And you probably keep things bottled up, too, don't you?"

She nodded. Jamal lifted her chin. "We're going to have to work on that."

"And just for the record, Nic and I don't have anything between us, and since I had to be honest with myself about him months ago, we never did have anything between us."

"We're not going to bring him up again unless it's in your office and we're talking about the jazz fest."

Michael backed out of his arms. "Shoot. I have to call the city about permits today. I'm glad you reminded me."

"Back to the real world."

"Yeah. But why don't you come by my place for dinner tonight? We can have cake for breakfast."

Jamal playfully swatted her backside. "Sounds like a plan."

After cleaning up the kitchen, Jamal and Michael went their separate ways. Jamal still couldn't help but wonder if there was more behind Michael's outburst about Nic. It had been a simple question. But he couldn't deny that he had a past and there were several women in Atlanta who could make a scene if they saw him and MJ out in public. He couldn't judge her for having a past, but it didn't stop him from being jealous as hell.

Michael walked into her office and sighed. She'd made a plum fool of herself at Jamal's over breakfast. He'd had a legitimate question, but she felt some kind of way when she was reminded about her one-sided relationship with Nic. She'd spent so much time hoping to prove that she was good enough for Nic and all she'd gotten in return was the ultimate kiss-off. She'd been hurt by it, but she was now over it. She just didn't understand why she'd gotten so upset this morning.

Was everything going to be different between them now? Would he want to have sex with her every time they saw each other now? Would they continue to explore restaurants and keep their friendship together, or would this be that friends-with-benefits thing that she was trying to avoid?

Picking up her desk phone, she called Mimi. Voice mail. Michael took that as a sign that she needed to figure this out on her own. Diving into work, she got most of the groundwork set for the jazz fest, securing permits for the venues and setting up meetings with the other clubs that would be participating in the festival.

Then she called Nic to see if he'd made any headway with the jazz mixer that they were going to use to promote the festival. As she listened to the phone ring,

Michael couldn't wait until this thing was over and she didn't have to deal with Nic anymore.

"Morning, Michael. You must have been reading my mind."

"Nic, I need to know when you're going to get that jazz compilation together and how long it will take to get it reproduced."

"All business, huh?"

"I'm not about to go back and forth with you today. I have a lot to do."

"Let's get together for lunch," he said. "I have some things to show you and it's a little early for me."

Michael sighed then looked at her calendar on her phone. "I can meet you at one thirty."

"Great. Why don't we go to that new café you like so much?"

"No. We can meet at Houston's on Lenox Road because I'll be coming from a meeting in that area."

"All right. Michael, is everything okay with you?"

"Everything is great. Thanks for asking."

"Why am I getting so much attitude from you?"

"Nic, you're not getting attitude. You're just not getting what you want."

"If things were that bad between us, why...? You know what? I'll see you at one thirty."

Michael was tempted to slam the phone down, but she hung up normally. Why had she wasted so much time with Nic when she'd known nothing good would come from it? Mimi had tried to warn her; hell, Nic had told her on several occasions that he wasn't trying to commit. But she'd stayed around hoping he would change his mind. Now she was shaken about this thing with Jamal.

What if Jamal changed his mind? What if he decided that he didn't want a commitment? And what about the other women? Could he be satisfied with one woman when he'd spent so many years dating many? If Michael was honest, it had been her fear that started the argument this morning. She needed to get over that. But how?

Rising from her seat, Michael looked out the window and decided that she was going to have to have faith in what she and Jamal had. She pulled her phone out of her pocket and sent him a text.

You just crossed my mind and I wanted to say hi.

Jamal smiled when he read MJ's text. Any other woman who would've sent a text like that would go on the do-not-call list. But Michael wasn't just any woman.

Thinking of you, too. Window is fixed. Going to email you the final security plan.

Okay. What do you have a taste for tonight?

Other than you? Surprise me.

Ha. Don't be nasty—right now. I'm still at work.

But you're the boss. I can come and have you for lunch later.

Damn, I have a meeting. Guess we'll have to wait for dinner.

Counting down the hours.

Jamal stuffed his phone in his pocket then hopped in his car. When he glanced in the rearview mirror, he saw Lucy's car.

"She's taking crazy to a whole new level," he muttered as he turned down a side road to see if she would follow. She did.

Then his phone rang.

"Yeah."

"I'm not stalking you. I just want to talk to you about last night."

"Lucy, we don't need to talk at all. You should just stop calling me, showing up at my place and following me."

"Jamal, I really care about you, and if…"

"Lucy. Lose. My. Number." Jamal hung up the phone and glanced in his rearview mirror to see if she was still following him. He started wondering if Lucy had been the deer who'd broken his window last night.

Michael glanced at her watch. She hated it when people were late without a call or email. Lucy Becker was pissing her off. Maybe Nic had been right about not wanting to work with her. If she didn't show up in the next five minutes, Michael was going to cut her from the list.

"Ms. Jane, Lucy Becker is here."

"Great. Send her in." *Late ass.*

Lucy walked into Michael's office looking like a glamorous jazz singer, rather than a club owner. She was supermodel-tall with a creamy caramel complexion and coal-black eyes. Michael was tempted to ask her if she could scat.

"Michael Jane, you are definitely not what I expected." Lucy extended her hand to her.

"I get that a lot. Lucy, thank you for coming in today."

"This jazz festival sounds like a great opportunity. What do you need me to do?"

Be on time. Michael smiled. "I want the jazz scene in Atlanta to come together and make this festival explode. You own one of the biggest clubs in the city. We wouldn't be able to put this on without you."

"That's true." Lucy smiled arrogantly. "What kind of groups are you booking to perform?"

"I'm leaving that to the experts like yourself and Nicolas Prince. Nic is actually in charge of getting the major acts together."

"No wonder you called me. That jackass doesn't know talent."

Michael stifled her laughter. Lucy, despite her lateness, might be all right. The women talked and laughed for about an hour before Lucy agreed to help with the jazz fest and start building a buzz about it at her club.

"Just one thing," she said as she grabbed her purse. "I want to make sure Nic knows he is not the only club owner sponsoring this. I hope that my place will benefit from some of this marketing and that I'm included in some of the after-hours events as well."

"Of course," Michael said.

Lucy smiled. "Great."

Once she was alone in her office, Michael wondered if all club owners were egomaniacs like Lucy and Nic. She'd find out when she met with the owner of Brown Sound Entertainment.

Dontae Brown was a pleasure to meet with, even if he was a bit of a flirt. He had been happy to throw his support behind the jazz fest and was even willing to help Nic host all the after-parties that he wanted. He'd kept asking Michael to join him for dinner, which she respectfully declined five times.

"You're the prettiest Michael I've ever met. At least take a selfie with me for Instagram."

"I can do that." She smiled as he held up his phone and snapped the picture. Then he kissed her on the cheek and took another photo.

"Team too much," she admonished.

"You kept telling me no. I had to steal a kiss."

"See you, Brown." Michael headed out the door. All she could do was hope her meeting with Nic would be quick and painless.

Jamal walked into Brent's office and caught him kissing his wife as if they were the only people in the world.

"Y'all keep this up, I'm going to be a godfather soon."

The couple broke their kiss then turned around and glared at Jamal. "Ever heard of knocking?" Brent asked.

"I did. I guess Mimi had her tongue in your ear and you didn't hear me."

"Shut up," Mimi said then threw a pen at Jamal. "Brent, I will see you in two days. Me, you and hot beignets."

"Keep talking like that and you'll see me on the plane with you." Brent kissed her one more time and Jamal turned away. Mimi and Brent made him smile and see that this was everything he wanted. He could see him and Michael having a relationship similar to this one, but there was no way he could let MJ live in another city even if she did commute back and forth. He needed her within arm's reach. Needed her lips against his in the morning, in the middle of the night, hell, right now.

"Hello," Brent said as he snapped his fingers in his friend's face. "What's wrong with you?"

Jamal smiled then waved goodbye to Mimi. When he and Brent were alone, Jamal sat down and smiled.

"I want that."

"You better define what *that* is, because if you're talking about my wife I'm going to have to punch you in your face."

"No, fool. I'm talking about what you and Mimi have. I think Michael and I can have that. I'm falling in love with her."

"Really? When did that happen?"

"Probably from the day I met her, but I know she feels the same way now, so I'm ready to settle down and be a one-woman man."

Brett looked out the window. "Has hell frozen over?

Are you serious? I mean, I hope you're right because if you hurt that woman I'm never gonna hear the end of it."

"Last night I realized that you don't need every woman in the world to be satisfied. You just need the right one, and MJ is the right one."

"Oh, shit, hell has frozen over."

Jamal shook his head. "I come to pour my heart out to you and you got jokes. I love this woman, or at least, I'm falling in love with her."

"What makes Michael different? I mean, how do you know that this is going to last? You need to know that before you get bored or get upset because Michael is Mimi's best friend. I can't get caught in the middle of one of your relationship mishaps."

"Have you ever heard me say this about a woman before? I'm always honest, and I'm going to be honest with Michael. I want her in my life for the long haul. I just got to make her believe that because I feel like, even though we have a connection, she's holding back."

"Maybe she has the same questions I have. Jamal, you've made it pretty clear that you don't want a serious relationship. Atlanta is your playground, right?"

"Used to be. I'm not playing a game with Michael."

"You better not be."

Jamal glared at his friend. "What? I can't change?"

"Just make sure this is real change and not you charming your way into Michael's pants."

Folding his arms across his chest, Jamal was starting to get angry. Though he could understand Brent's line of thinking. "Trust me when I say this—Michael is more than a woman I want to sleep with. We've stargazed."

Brent eyed his friend incredulously. "If you told her your astronaut story, then I might believe you."

"Told her the story, showed her Orion and explained the Big Dipper to her."

"Yep. Hell has frozen over. You're in love."

"I need your help. Find out from Mimi what the real deal is with MJ and Nic. When we met earlier this week, dude was acting like a jealous ex, and he was telling her that I come to his place to pick up women."

"Well, you do."

Jamal shot Brent an icy look. "Used to. I'm not trying to be her rebound if there is still something between them." He told Brent about the disagreement he and MJ had this morning.

Brent laughed at the end of the story. "I'm surprised she didn't punch you in the face. You, of all people, should never question a woman about her past. If she did that to you, which she has the right to do, you would be pissed off."

"There isn't a woman in this city that I'm working with and we've had a past anything."

"Oh, so you're jealous?"

"Don't be silly. I'm Jamal Carver. I don't do jealousy."

Brent laughed. "You're doing a good job of it right now. Your eyes are turning green like the Hulk."

"Shut up."

"Come on. I'll let you buy me lunch and listen to how you're not jealous." The two men headed for the door and decided to hit one of their favorite restaurants from their college days: Houston's.

"I hope they still have the purple cabbage," Jamal said as they walked to his car.

Chapter 9

What is this? Keep Michael Waiting Day? she thought as she sat in Houston's waiting for Nic.

When the waiter came over to refresh her glass of water, Michael looked up at the entrance and saw Nic kissing some young woman.

She smiled, thinking, *Good for him. Maybe now he can mind his business and stay out of my life.*

Then he shooed the woman away and made his way over to the table where Michael was sitting. "Hi. Sorry I'm late. Was a little busy."

"No problem, but a call or text would've been nice," Michael said. "I do have other things to do, but I have made a lot of headway with the jazz fest. We should be good for October, maybe November."

"November's the holiday season. People aren't going

to want to spend money on tickets when they have to buy Christmas gifts and turkey dinners to bake."

MJ shook her head. "Your timeline is a little ridiculous if we're going to market this right and make this a successful event. If you just want to put together some random jazz groups and call it a festival, why are you working me so hard?"

Nic leaned back in his seat and smiled. "I hope you're not giving me attitude because of what you just saw."

"Unlike you, Nic, I couldn't care less about what you do with your personal life. But what I do care about is you showing up twenty minutes late for a one-thirty meeting when I've been running around all day talking to all of these club owners so that we can get the jazz fest going. You may have been getting busy, but you weren't working on what's important."

"Excuse me. I appreciate all the work you're doing, and despite what you think, I have been working. The promotional compilation will be ready tomorrow. And I sent you an email with some different art ideas."

"Great." Michael reached into her purse and handed Nic a proposal that she'd drawn up after her meeting with Lucy and Brown.

"You have been busy." He flipped through the pages. "Lucy really wants to be a part of this? Not surprised that she wants some events at her place. She is a lunatic."

"Well, she thinks you're a jackass." Michael picked up her glass of water and took a sip. Nic rolled his eyes and continued reading.

"Why do you want to move the date to October? All

of this stuff can be done and we can have it on Labor Day, like I want."

"And having a new Labor Day event means we're going to have a lot of competition. Established events that people go to every year. Had we had more time, we could've put together the event for August and branded it as end of summer. But we'll have to do it next year. It's October or nothing if you want this event to go well. We just need to make sure all of the groups you've lined up are able to perform."

"As long as I get the contracts signed, we're good."

"Well, as long as you deliver the artists, then I think we can produce the best fall jazz festival that will blow the city away."

"I just have one concern," Nic said. "What about security? You can't still want to use First Line of Defense after the lawsuit and everything."

Michael gritted her teeth. "Yes, I'm still using First Line of Defense because they're good at what they do. If you paid attention to the news, you'd see that they had nothing to do with what happened in the parking lot."

"And this has nothing to do with the fact that you're sleeping with the head of the security firm?"

"Assuming things again. Check their record. They have handled security for some of the biggest events in the city. We'd be stupid not to use them."

"I'm not crazy about using a security firm that's caught up in bad publicity. And I still don't like the metal detectors. We're going for a more mature crowd. Detectors are going to offend a lot of the people."

MJ shifted in her seat. "Do you want to be liable if

there is an incident because we didn't have metal detectors? Also, insurance will be a lot cheaper if we have more security measures in place."

From the look on Nic's face, she knew she had him. "All right. I guess the metal detectors will be what we do. I still don't like them."

"At this point, it's not about what you like. It's about what's best for the safety of the people who will be attending the event. So are we done here?"

"You got a point, even if you're trying to have a lunch meeting without lunch."

"I wasn't late—you were. But if I'm honest, I'm hungry, too."

Smiling, Nic patted the back of her hand and picked up a menu. "Since you've worked so hard, I'll even spring for lunch."

"As if you had a choice."

Brent knew something was wrong the moment he saw Jamal's fist clench. Then he followed his friend's gaze and saw Michael and Nic sitting at a table. Jamal turned to Brent. "Let's go someplace else."

"No. Now you got me wanting cabbage and a Biltmore. You really think that's more than a business lunch?"

"The hell does it look like to you? Is he holding her hand and she's letting him? What part of a business lunch is that?" Jamal narrowed his eyes at them.

"Look, she just snatched her hand away and doesn't even know you're stalking her." Brent chuckled. "I'm actually glad Mimi isn't here to see this. I wouldn't be able to stop her from writing about this and I wouldn't try."

"I'm going to speak to them."

"Do not make a scene. You still have to work with that man, and MJ doesn't strike me as a woman who likes drama played out in public."

"He looks like he wants to put her on a plate."

"Stop projecting and staring at them. If this is you in love, I'm scared."

"Shut up."

"If you're going to go over there, be an adult."

"Don't judge me." Jamal crossed over to MJ and Nic. "Hello, guys."

MJ smiled as if she was happy to see him, but Jamal noticed Nic's scowl.

"What are you doing here?" she asked as she rose to her feet and kissed him on the cheek.

"Mimi went back to New Orleans today and Brent is depressed."

Nic snorted. "I find that hard to believe. That man is probably celebrating."

MJ speared him with an icy look and Jamal had the common sense to hold back his caustic comment. "This was the work study restaurant back in the day."

"Yes. Because the spinach dip is to die for," MJ said.

Nic cleared his throat. "Maybe we should order one."

"Good idea. You guys enjoy. MJ, I'll see you later." Jamal walked away without saying another word to Nic. If that wasn't being adult, he didn't know what was.

Brent shook his head as Jamal returned to the front door, where they'd been waiting for a table. "No yelling and no glasses thrown. Looks like you're not as scary as I thought."

"Want to know what he said about your wife?"

"That mother..."

"No, no, you have to be an adult." Jamal shook his head. "I don't know what she ever saw in him."

"Does it matter? She's with you."

"Yeah. Let's get this cabbage and get out of here before I forget that she's mine."

Michael tried to focus on whatever Nic was saying, but her eyes kept wandering over to where Brent and Jamal were sitting. Jamal seemed to know it, too, because when their eyes met he'd lick the tortilla chip, reminding her what his tongue could do.

"Hello? Are you listening to me?"

Michael focused on Nic's face. "No."

"My God, you really are sleeping with him."

"Didn't you spend part of your afternoon doing that with the young lady you brought here earlier? And for the last time, my personal life is none of your business."

"You have your finger on the nuclear bomb, but if that's what..."

"Shut up."

Nic shook his head. "I'm done."

"Thank you."

After they ordered, Nic received a phone call and excused himself from the table. "Hey," Michael said. "Lunch is on you, remember."

He opened his wallet and handed her two twenties

then dashed out the door. Michael was alone for only a few seconds.

"Excuse me, pretty lady? Is this seat taken?"

"It will be if you sit down, Jamal."

"Where did Mr. Personality go?" he asked as he sank into the chair across from her.

Michael shrugged. "Got a phone call and ran out of here. Did you dump Brent?"

"I wish. He's coming over here after he gets the last bit of spinach dip out of that bowl."

"So, do I have time to lean over for a kiss?"

Jamal nodded and gave her the kiss they'd both wanted since they saw each other moments ago.

"My God, people trying to eat. Get a room."

"Don't be a hater because your wife is gone." Jamal licked his lips and winked at Michael.

"My wife will be back in two days. Don't make me be that annoying friend that hangs out with you the whole time she's gone."

Michael laughed. "You can't do that, Brent. I'm sorry we have plans."

Brent smiled at the happy couple. "I'm sure you do. So how is the jazz-festival planning for you guys? All work and no play or a lot of play and a little bit of work?"

"It's coming along. At least we have a great security plan in place. I met with some clubs on this today, and corralling them all together is going to be interesting." She stroked her forehead. "But I think we can make it work."

"Who did you meet with?" Jamal asked.

Michael took a sip of water. "Dontae Brown and Lucy Becker."

Jamal nearly choked on his water. "Lucy Becker? She's nuts."

"And obviously doesn't own a watch. She was so late for our meeting, and that is my number one pet peeve. Why do you say she's nuts?"

Brent stifled a laugh. Michael looked from Brent to Jamal.

"Is anyone going to let me in on the joke?"

Jamal nodded. "We went out once."

"Really?"

"You'd think I'd broken off our engagement when I told her that I wasn't going to see her anymore."

Michael took a gulp of water. Lucy was beautiful, she seemed smart and she couldn't hold Jamal's attention?

"Don't give me that look," he said.

"What look would that be?"

"The 'I can't believe you've dated half of the women in Atlanta' look?" Brent quipped. Jamal turned to his friend and glared at him.

"Not. Helping."

Michael set her glass down and threw her hands up. "I was just drinking water. Besides, we all have a past."

"And she's probably going to try and angle to turn this into a reality show. That seems to be the new thing for mildly successful women in Atlanta."

"Tell me about it," Brent snorted.

"Don't tell me Mimi is…"

Brent shook his head. "No. She is happy being behind the computer screen with her blog. But I dated a woman who thought we should've allowed our relationship to play out on a *Real Housewives of Atlanta* type of show."

Jamal laughed. "Denisha Tate, God bless her gold-digging soul. I heard she has landed a show."

"Seriously?"

"*Looking for Love in Hot-lanta.* They contacted FLD about doing security for the show last week."

Michael scoffed. "That show is going to be a hot mess. I can't believe people want to air their dirty laundry for the world to see. That stuff never goes away. I hope Mimi doesn't write about it."

"Me, too," Brent said.

"Oh, does Mimi not know about Denisha?" Jamal asked. "I know…"

"Shut up, Jamal. There's no need for Mimi to know about a failed relationship of mine." He held up his left hand. "We already put rings on it."

Michael began to wonder if she wanted to know more about Jamal's failed relationship with Lucy. Did it matter? They were together and working on their future. Was his past really that important? She mentally shrugged it off. They were going to look forward, not backward.

Once the waiter brought their food over, including another spinach dip, the trio fell into a casual conversation.

"This was fun," Brent said as he glanced at his watch. "But I have to get back to work."

"And you need to pay for your food." Jamal extended his hand to his friend. Brent shook his head.

"Lunch is still on you even if I didn't have to listen to you lament over your...problems."

Michael raised her eyebrow. "Problems?"

"Pay him no mind. I'll get you, Brent. Wait until Mimi comes home."

"You two are horrible." Michael laughed then wiped her mouth. "I have to go as well. Need to get some reports together for this jazz fest and check on a couple of my other clients. I'll be glad when the show is over."

"Me, too," Jamal muttered. Brent waved goodbye to the couple and headed out the door. Jamal stood up and wrapped his arms around Michael's waist.

"This was a pleasant surprise and I'm glad we had this lunch meeting. But you're not off the hook for dinner. I'm thinking a sushi buffet all over your body."

Michael kissed him on the cheek. "Why are you so nasty?"

"Because you like it. See you tonight."

As MJ walked out of the restaurant, Jamal's mind filled with questions about Lucy. Was she angling to work with MJ because she knew they were involved? *She can't know that, but I know when she finds out she's probably going to go off the deep end.*

Calling her was out of the question, and how did he warn MJ without seeming like the playboy she thought he was? The only person he could really talk to was the woman who'd told him to settle down a long time ago. His gran.

"Jamal, what did I do to get an unexpected call from

you? You better not be calling about not finding fresh crawfish."

"I'm starting to feel like you've branded me because you ate that one bad crawfish in the bunch."

"Boy, you know that mess was frozen. Anyway, how are you doing today, grandson?"

"I have to tell you something."

"Please don't tell me you've gotten someone pregnant and you're going to have to marry her because you're not going to let her take your son away from you."

Jamal blinked rapidly. "Are you sure you weren't a writer in a past life? I said I have something to tell you and you've given me a crazy baby mama that I have to marry to keep my kid and you're just assuming it's going to be a boy?"

"What do you have to tell me?"

Jamal laughed. "I think I've met the one."

"Lord, these are the end of days. Jamal, you're really going to get married?"

"Slow down, Gran. We're not there, yet. But Michael is…"

"Did you say 'Michael'? Baby, I didn't know you were gay. I love you just the same and I want you to know we will welcome Michael into the family and celebrate your union because love is love."

"Gran, Michael is a woman. I'm not gay and when you meet her she can explain her name to you. Listen, how do I get MJ to take me seriously and realize that I'm not the cad that people seem to think I am?"

"Jamal, I've always told you that you can't play with women like they are interchangeable Barbie dolls."

"I don't do that." Jamal could imagine his grandmother scoffing at him. "Okay, maybe I did that in the past. But according to you, that's a family trait."

"And I had to break your grandfather from that. You know how? I made him miss me. I left him and he had to learn that I wasn't the kind of woman you could find every day. You better treat her that way now."

"What about the woman I want to leave me alone?"

"Call the police and keep her away from your new woman. Jamal, actions speak louder than words."

"You're right. I love you, Gran."

"I know you do. And you're sure Michael is a girl?"

"One hundred percent."

"All right. Can't wait to meet her."

Jamal couldn't help but laugh when he hung up with his grandmother. Still, he worried that Lucy might cause a serious problem in his budding relationship with MJ.

Chapter 10

Michael was ready to call it a day, but she had one client who needed to be talked through how to use Instagram to market her new line of coffee-infused cupcakes. A fifteen-minute conversation turned into a two-hour workshop. By the time she got off the phone with the baker, Michael knew she needed to hire a social-media guru to handle these things in the future.

"It costs to be the boss." She shut down her computer and placed her phone system on night answer because she wasn't taking another phone call today. Glancing at her watch, she realized that whatever she had planned for dinner wasn't going to work now. She hoped Jamal would enjoy takeout from the Sunshine Café. When she made it outside, she noticed that Lucy was coming her way. *Not now*, she thought as she plastered a smile on her face.

"Michael, I'm glad I caught you." Lucy stood in front of her like an imposing linebacker from the Falcons. "I have a great idea on how we can get more eyes on the festival."

"Awesome. But can it wait until tomorrow? I have dinner plans that I'm running late for."

"Oh, well, I guess. But it will only take a second."

Michael glanced at her watch and sighed. "What is it?"

"One of my dearest friends produces some docuseries for a popular network, and I was telling her about my involvement with this event. She wants to follow me around and film the preparations."

Michael laughed inwardly. Brent and Jamal had been right. "We're talking a reality show?"

"That's what some people call them, but it's really a look into my life, and Nic is on board with it."

"Of course he is."

"But you're the marketing genius and I wanted to get your input. From what I understand, some of the best and brightest of Atlanta is going to be a part of the festival. The world should see what we're about, you know."

"Why don't you send me some details about the show and I'll see if it is a fit for what we're doing. Then we need to make sure everyone involved is all right with being filmed and get waivers."

"Great. I know this has the potential to be golden. Are you available for a breakfast meeting?"

"I'll have to check my schedule and let you know. Lucy, I really have to go."

"Okay. 'Bye, Michael."

Getting into her car, Michael shook her head. She couldn't wait for this festival to be over. How many more months did they have to go?

After ordering dinner and grabbing a bottle of wine, Michael was finally ready to head home. She hated that she didn't have the view of the sky that Jamal had over at his place. But she had a different view she was ready to show him. She reached her place with just enough time to plate their dinners and change into something that would make Jamal see all kinds of stars.

Jamal paid for the two dozen roses and tipped the florist for unlocking the door for him when he arrived. "Next time, I'll come earlier."

"Please do. But thank you." She counted the money and was very impressed with the tip. Jamal headed to his car and sped down the midtown streets. He couldn't wait to see MJ, kiss her and wrap his arms around her.

He was going to listen to Gran and let MJ know she was the only woman he wanted and needed. Jamal just hoped that Lucy wouldn't be a problem. When he was alone, her quasi-stalking hadn't been a problem. Now he didn't want MJ to be in harm's way. He glanced in his rearview mirror to see if Lucy was lurking in the shadows. So far, so good.

Arriving at MJ's, Jamal wasn't thinking about Lucy anymore. He was yearning to see Michael and feel her arms around him. She opened the door before he rang the bell, and when he took a look at her, he nearly dropped the roses in his hand.

Michael stood there in a V-neck red lace teddy that accented her creamy skin and hugged her amazing curves. "Damn."

"I have to apologize. I got off late and didn't have time to cook." She ushered him into the house. "We have takeout from Sunshine Café."

Jamal nodded but couldn't take his eyes off her hips and those legs as she glided across the floor. "MJ."

When she turned around with a smile on her cherry-red lips, Jamal forgot what he was going to say. She touched his hand and took the roses.

"These are for me, right?"

"Yes. And I couldn't care less about dinner, whether you put these roses in water or anything other than those shoes on my shoulders." When she dropped the roses on the counter, Jamal grabbed her and kissed her slow and deep. MJ wrapped one leg around his waist and he felt her heat. And when she thrust her hips into him, Jamal was harder than a ton of bricks. Walking toward the sofa, he laid her on the soft cushions and spread her legs apart. She put those shoes on his shoulders as he pulled the crotch of her teddy to the side and licked her sweet nectar. So wet. So good. She arched her hips up to his lips, allowing him to go deeper inside her. Jamal devoured her, finding her throbbing bud and sucking it until she screamed his name.

He needed to feel her wetness around his hardness. Pulling back from his goddess, Jamal stripped out of his clothes. "You're so beautiful when you're satisfied."

"Then you're the best-kept beauty secret in the world."

"Let's take this to your bedroom. Show me the way." Jamal lifted her into his arms and MJ pointed to the top of the stairs.

"To the left."

Jamal headed into the room she pointed to and laid her on the bed. She looked so alluring on the lavender bedspread. He placed the palm of his hand in the center of her chest. MJ's skin felt like silk. He stroked her hard nipples with his fingertips and she moaned. Jamal leaned in and licked her nipples. "Yes," MJ exclaimed. "Yes."

He slipped his hand between her thighs and stroked her wetness until she hummed. "Jamal. Need. You."

He needed her even more, but he didn't have protection right then. As if she could read his mind, MJ reached underneath her pillow and handed him a condom. "I was a Girl Scout." She winked at him as he tore the package open.

Jamal slid the condom in place then dived into her wetness. "Michael!" They ground against each other at a hurried pace. She tightened her thighs against him and Jamal nearly climaxed. But he pressed on, pushing deeper and deeper inside her until she came down like a summer rain. And when her wetness dripped on him, Jamal exploded like a cherry bomb.

Collapsing in each other's arms, the duo closed their eyes and released a sigh of release.

"Amazing," Michael said.

Jamal kissed her cheek. "Yes, you were."

"Sorry about dinner."

"What are you apologizing for? This was the best dinner I could've had. You worked a lot this week."

"I know, and when I was leaving, Lucy showed up pitching her reality-show idea."

Jamal went still. Did Lucy know about him and MJ? "Was that all she wanted?"

"Doesn't matter. I know what I want. More of you." MJ brushed her lips against his neck. "Think we can have round two, then dinner?"

"Sounds like a great plan."

After making love again for another hour, MJ and Jamal headed downstairs to eat their cold dinner. Jamal was glad MJ had covered her amazing body with a white cotton dress so that he could focus on his dinner.

"Jambalaya pie." She set the plate in front of him and all Jamal wanted was for her to be on that plate. It didn't matter what MJ wore—he wanted her. He wrapped his arms around her waist.

"How about another helping of that Michael Jane pie?" He licked his lips and squeezed her ample bottom.

"You are too much. We do have to work tomorrow."

"That's like fourteen hours away from now." He winked at her and pulled her closer to his chest. "You're beautiful."

"You keep telling me that. I guess I should start believing you."

"Yes, you should. MJ, I want you to know that you're one of the best parts of my life. I've never felt this way about anyone before."

She touched her forehead against his. "You don't have to tell me what you think I want to hear."

"I don't say anything I don't mean." Jamal captured her lips in a hot kiss. She melted in his arms and Jamal knew Michael was the one woman he couldn't live without.

Michael pulled back from Jamal and smiled. "I'm so hungry. And I need my energy if you want some more of this pie."

"Please, eat."

A comfortable silence enveloped them as they ate, and Michael couldn't help but stare at him and wonder if this was really going to work. She couldn't crave him this much, put her heart out there and hope that he didn't hurt her. Of course, this man wasn't Nic. He was with her because of her and not what she could do for him.

"What's that look about?"

"What look?" Michael smiled. "Can't I enjoy eye candy?"

"I feel like a piece of meat," he quipped.

"I could bite you. Jamal, this is fun. I like being with you."

He inched closer to her. "So do I. MJ, I want you to know this—you're the only woman who means anything to me. I've never known anyone like you. When I wake up in the morning, you're the first thing on my mind. I look forward to hearing your voice, seeing your face and feeling your lips against mine."

MJ's heart swelled and she struggled not to let the tears welling up in her eyes fall. Jamal cupped her cheek.

"Are you sure you're ready for just one woman in your life?" Her voice was low. He brushed his lips across hers.

"As long as that one woman is you, then yes."

Chapter 11

Michael woke up in Jamal's arms. She wished she could stay there all day but she had work to do. When he tightened his arms around her waist, she decided work could wait and snuggled closer to him.

"Morning." The heat from his breath sent tingles down her spine.

"Morning." She turned to face him.

"How are you this beautiful in the morning? Where's the drool?"

She elbowed him in his stomach. "I don't drool, thank you very much."

"That hurt, woman!"

"Want me to kiss it and make it better?"

"Yes. But if you do that, we're not getting out of this bed today." Jamal glanced at the clock on her nightstand. "And I have a meeting this morning with the producers of that show."

"You're going to do security for them?"

"Depends on the type of show it is. I have some guys who would be excited about pulling fighting women apart. Don't all of those shows have some sort of cat-fighting?"

She shrugged. "I try not to watch those shows. They make women look like man-hungry idiots."

Jamal laughed. "Guessing you have no desire to star in one."

"Not at all. All publicity isn't good publicity—I don't care what people say. If you want to build a brand and develop a name for yourself, the best way to do it is hard work. Do you think Oprah would do a reality show?"

"Hell no. But she's Oprah."

"That's right, and hard work made her Oprah."

"That's what you want? To be like Oprah?"

Michael sighed. "No, I just want to have a legacy that I can be proud of. My family was poor, but proud. That's the reason my mother never fixed my name on my birth certificate."

"Wow."

"It's opened some doors for me. Your friend even thought I was a man."

Jamal raised his eyebrow. "My friend?"

"Lucy."

He scoffed. "She isn't my friend. More like an annoyance."

"Are you sure that's all she is?"

Jamal nodded. "And how about this—you're naked in

my arms. Why are we talking about another woman?" Before she could answer, Jamal captured her lips in a hot, wet kiss. Michael pressed her body against his, feeling his hardness grow against her thighs. She opened her legs, inviting him to her wetness. Just as he was about to enter her, both of their cell phones began ringing.

"Ignore it," he moaned. "Work can wait."

Her silent agreement was when she thrust her hips into his. Protection was the last thing on his mind as Jamal reveled in her wetness. He thrust deeper and deeper inside her. Michael's moans were like a symphony of bliss. The skin-to-skin connection was just delicious. Reckless. So damned good. Jamal tried to hold back his explosive climax, tried to keep himself from giving in to pleasure. But Michael felt so good and he couldn't hold off any longer. She dug her nails into his shoulder as the ripples of her orgasm attacked her body.

"Whoa," she said when she caught her breath. "That's a good way to start the morning."

"Best part of waking up." Jamal winked at her. "Going forward, we're going to have to be more careful."

Michael nodded. "I'm on the pill but nothing is one hundred percent."

"And in case you're wondering, I get tested often for work and I don't have any STIs."

"Good—me either. Still, we're too old to be this irresponsible."

Jamal glanced at Michael's belly, watching a bead of sweat roll down it. What if his careless action made them parents? Normally, he'd be filled with fear and loathing, but he wouldn't mind raising a child with MJ. Watching her belly grow with his little boy and going to get her weird snacks. He even smiled at the image of him in a pair of green scrubs holding her hand as she gave birth to Jamal Jr. Or maybe they would name him Michael as well.

"What's going through that head?" She stroked his cheek.

"Nothing. Just enjoying the view."

"We'd better get out of this bed and go be adults. Run our businesses and whatnot." Michael propped herself up on her elbows and kissed Jamal's collarbone. Neither of them made an effort to move. It took another thirty minutes for them to break their embrace and get ready for work.

Leaving Michael's bed was probably the hardest thing that Jamal had to do. If she'd wanted to play hooky, he would've sent someone else to meet with the producers of the show. But MJ had to be responsible. He loved that about her. Loved a lot of things about her. He was super close to falling in love with her. That scared him a little bit and excited him as well. *Get it together and get some work done.* Jamal picked up his phone to check his missed calls and text messages. When he saw Lucy's number, he wanted to toss his phone out the window.

Miss you so much. Can we talk and see if we can work things out?

The next message from Lucy was angrier. So, you're just going to ignore me? I guess you have some whore in your bed tonight! I'll forgive you, but you have to talk to me.

Jamal deleted the messages and blocked Lucy's number. Hopefully, he wouldn't have to deal with her while MJ helped plan this jazz fest. He was glad that he'd taken his gran's advice and shown MJ that she was the only woman he needed and wanted. Jamal was confident that they would have a great future together.

Then he called the producer back and told him that he was running late for the meeting but he'd be there.

"No worries. We're actually meeting with cast right now and it ran over. I'm glad you're not sitting in the lobby waiting."

"Awesome." Jamal slowed down a bit as he drove. Since things weren't on schedule, he didn't have to rush. Any other day, he'd be pissed because he would've been sitting out there in the lobby waiting with an attitude.

Michael floated into the office and didn't care that she was the one late for the meeting with Nic. She would've called, but she hadn't felt the need to do so. Nic had kept her waiting so many times and turnabout was fair play.

"Well, it's about time." Nic rose to his feet when he saw Michael crossing the lobby.

"Traffic."

"I called you this morning."

"Talking and driving is very dangerous. Come on— let's get started." Michael walked toward her office, giving a nod and a smile to her receptionist. Once she and Nic entered her office, Michael took her seat and smiled at him.

"What can I help you with this morning?"

Nic rolled his eyes and handed Michael a CD. "You made it seem as if getting this mix done was a priority."

"This is great." She inserted the disc in her computer and turned the speakers on. The sweet sounds of jazz filled the room and Michael swayed in her seat. She knew this was a CD she'd play the next time she and Jamal got together.

"She likes it." Nic extended his hand to Michael as an upbeat song came on.

"I don't think so."

"Come on. This is the hit from the compilation and your reaction is proof of that. Let's dance."

Michael gave in to the beat and danced with Nic. Once upon a time, Nic and Michael were the king and queen of salsa. As they danced, neither of them noticed Lucy standing in the doorway snapping pictures on her cell phone until the song ended.

"Well, you two are very cozy." Lucy walked in and sat down across from Michael's desk. Nic shook his head and Michael walked over to the computer to turn the music off.

"This is the mix that we're going to use to promote the jazz festival," Michael said. "It sounds great."

"I see. I had no idea I was walking into a dance party. I would've worn different shoes."

"Anyway," Nic said. "I have about five thousand copies printed. They're being delivered to all of the participating clubs. And we have permits for all of the outdoor locations that we want to hold performances at. Ladies, we are good to go." He placed a folder on Michael's desk.

"Almost," Michael interjected as she took a seat. "We need to get the security details for each location. So, I'm going to talk to Jamal about sending folks out to get a..."

"Jamal Carver?" Lucy asked.

"Yes. First Line of Defense is handling security for the event."

"They are a good group. Jamal is pretty awesome."

Nic sucked his teeth. "Why don't y'all start a fan club for the guy?"

"Jealous, Nic?" Lucy quipped. "I'm sure you're the president of your own fan club."

"And you're the queen of yours."

Michael hid her smile. She hadn't seen anyone get under Nic's skin like this except Mimi. Maybe Lucy wasn't as bad as Jamal said she was. Maybe.

"Are we done here?" Michael rose from her seat. "I want to get these locations to Jamal so that we can start getting the security plan in place."

"Oh, I can do that," Lucy said with a smile. She held her hand out for the file Nic had given Michael.

"I got this."

Lucy's face hardened for a minute, leading Michael to believe that Jamal may have been right about her. At any rate, she wanted everyone out of her office.

"This has been great, but I have another meeting in about ten minutes."

"With Jamal?" Lucy asked. Nic shot her a questioning look as Michael shook her head.

"I do have other clients. So, we're done, right?"

Lucy cleared her throat and stood up. "Yes, we are. When can I expect to have these CDs in my club?"

"They're being delivered now," Nic said. "Mikey, thanks for the dance." As he headed out the door, Michael wanted to throw something at him. But she was happy to see him and Lucy leave. She picked up her phone and sent Jamal a text.

Hope your meeting went better than mine.

Jamal shook hands with the reality-show producer, who said, "I look forward to our partnership."

"Me, too," Jamal said. "I'm going to have my crew come over tomorrow and introduce themselves to you and the ladies."

"Sounds good. Too bad you won't be around. You could get some scene time and send hearts racing."

"I'm good with that." Jamal pulled his phone out of his pocket and smiled at MJ's message. "Have a good day."

Meeting was great. Sorry you didn't have the same experience. Want me to kiss it and make it better?

You bet. Lunch?

You're on the menu?

That can be arranged.

See you at one?

Cool.

Glancing at his watch, Jamal saw that he had time to go to his office and get his crew together to head to the production office. He missed Harry, because he would've put him in charge of this assignment.

Had he acted in haste when he fired him? When he arrived at his office, he called Harry. Voice mail. He wondered if his old friend and colleague was salty about the firing. "Hey, Harry, this is Jamal. Give me a call when you get this. We need to talk."

After hanging up the phone, he called his staff in to tell them about the new assignment. Jamal had no problem finding guys who wanted to work on the reality-show set. Because he knew men could be distracted by some of Atlanta's sexiest women, he decided to put Diana Jones in charge of the group.

"Really?" she asked.

"Yes. You're ready. We're going to get started next week and it runs for eight weeks. Each one of you will have to sign an agreement saying that you won't talk about the show or reveal the winner." Jamal pointed at his team. "You guys are going to have to go to the studio and get your credentials and sign those contracts."

"Guess this means we're back!" Marcel Carpenter exclaimed.

"Yes. We've been cleared in the lawsuit. We're also

under contract to work a jazz festival later this year. So, it looks as if we are back."

Everyone cheered and Jamal held his hands up. "Since we have these big contracts coming up, we have to be on point."

The crew nodded in agreement. "That's all," Jamal said. "Thank you guys for all of your hard work."

As the meeting ended, Jamal couldn't help but smile. He loved his crew and was sure that they were going to rock out both events. As he glanced at his watch, his smile got even bigger. It was time to go see Michael.

Michael wanted to bang her head against her desk after her meeting with the most computer-illiterate business owner in Atlanta. This man had no idea about social media and marketing his restaurant on it. Trying to explain Twitter and Facebook to the sixty-year-old felt like pulling teeth. But after two hours, she'd finally gotten him to get it. By the time he left, Michael had set up his social-media accounts and he had a couple of hundred followers already.

She was glad that she could hand this account off to one of her social-media mavens. Just as she was about to head to the bathroom to freshen her makeup, the receptionist buzzed her.

"Mr. Carver is here to see you."

Michael looked at her watch. He was early. "Send him in."

Jamal strode into the office, crossing over to Michael and pulling her into his arms. He didn't say hello, just captured her mouth in a hot kiss. She melted in his arms and returned his kiss with fervor. Their tongues danced a sensual tango and she was tempted to push everything off her desk and make love to him right there. Jamal tore his mouth away from hers and smiled.

"Better?"

"Much."

Jamal stroked her cheek. "Sorry your meeting sucked."

Michael groaned. "Lucy and Nic are two hardheaded people. Then I had a meeting with a new client who didn't even know what Facebook was. It's been an afternoon. Thank goodness for the amazing morning I had with you." She winked at him. "So, what's for lunch?"

"If I'm not mistaken, it's you—right?"

"And that's a good thing for you, but I'm hungry." She thrust her hip into him.

"Then if you want something to eat, you better not do that again. Want to order in? I have some questions for you about the security plan for the jazz fest."

"I need to get away from this desk." *Because if we stay in here, we might just end up on top of it.*

"All right. Let's get out of here."

Michael grabbed her purse and Jamal took her hand in his. "Ready to ride fast?"

"Why don't you hand me the keys and let me show you how fast works." Michael held out her hand. "One of the first things I ever wanted from you was to drive the fastback Mustang."

"Using me for my car. I feel so cheap." Jamal placed the key in her hand. "Be gentle with her."

Michael shook her head. "What is it about you men and your cars?"

"The control, the power and the beauty. It's like a woman."

"You should stop while you're behind."

"Yes, ma'am."

When they arrived at the car, Michael smiled. "Well, she is beautiful."

"Wait until you feel her power."

She slid in the driver's seat and cranked the car as Jamal got into the passenger side. The roar of the engine gave her a thrill. "How many tickets have you gotten in this car?"

"I'm going to plead the Fifth. But let's just say I don't drive through Paulding County anymore."

MJ pressed her foot on the gas pedal and tore out of the parking lot. "Yes!"

Jamal gripped his seat belt as if he was about to be tossed out of the car. "Guess you're going to get banned from Fulton County."

She slowed down a bit. "That's not going to happen. Where do you want to eat?"

"There's this barbecue joint in East Point that will give you a chance to open Sally up on the highway."

"You named your car Sally?"

Jamal grinned. "She has her own theme song."

"And let me guess—you have it on your smartphone."

Jamal leaned over and turned the radio on. The sounds of Wilson Pickett filled the car. Jamal and Michael began singing to the legend's voice. When they passed a Georgia State Patrol car, Michael slowed down.

"I see why you're banned in Paulding County. This car is awesome."

"The driver is much better." He placed his hand on her thigh.

"I always wanted a Mustang, but I figured it would be too hard to put a car seat and a diaper bag in."

"Really? But you don't have kids."

Michael sighed and tightened her grip on the steering wheel. "Let's just say when I planned my life, I thought I'd have a couple of kids by now."

Jamal glanced out the window and didn't say a word. Michael noted his silence and sighed. "You know how it goes. We make plans and God laughs."

"Who did you imagine as the father of these paper babies?"

"Doesn't matter because my life has taken a different direction and I'm pretty happy with it."

"That's a good thing."

"A great thing." She smiled. "So, where am I going?"

"Next exit."

She nodded and took the exit. Jamal directed her to the small restaurant at the end of a one-lane road.

"How did you find this place?"

"On a drive one day about six months ago. They have the best coleslaw in the metro area."

"How do you eat all of this food and not gain a pound?" She gave him a slow once-over as she parked the car.

"Gym time. And you have been avoiding that challenge. It ends today."

She rolled her eyes. "Fine. But you're going to lose."

"Talk is cheap. So, what do I get when I win?"

Michael broke out into laughter. "Since you're not going to win, the question is, what do I get?"

"Anything you want."

"This car for a week?"

"Anything but that."

"No fair!"

"What about I cook dinner for you for a month?"

She shook her head. "I just want to drive Sally for a week."

"Fine. And when I win, you become my personal chef for a week."

Michael extended her hand to him. "You're on."

They got out of the car and headed inside. The restaurant was rustic and small. The tables were wooden like old school picnic benches. Jamal pointed to a round table in the back. "Let's sit there."

"No hostess?"

He smirked and shook his head. "Come on, woman. You know better." They walked over to the table, and seconds later, a tall woman in a stained apron walked over to them.

"Jamal! Where have you been?"

"Working." He stood and hugged the older woman. "But I have been missing this place."

"I know you have. Bet you haven't had a pulled-pork sandwich—a good one, anyway—in months."

"You're right about that." Jamal turned to Michael. "This is my girlfriend, MJ."

"Well. This is nice. Come on, girl. Give me a hug!"

Michael stood up and hugged the woman. "It's about time he brought a lady friend around here."

MJ smiled. "He says this place is amazing."

"Telling the truth and nothing but the truth. Please tell me you're not one of those vegan women."

"I'm not. Hanging with this guy would make it hard to be one of those."

"Good. I have an idea for what y'all need to eat. A sampler platter."

Jamal gave her a thumbs-up. "Sounds good! Extra coleslaw."

The woman shook her head and walked into the kitchen. After Jamal and MJ settled in their seats, she looked at him and smiled. "You seem at home here."

"Miss Lizzy reminds me of my auntie from Savannah. Good food, advice whether you want it or not and more food."

MJ placed her hand on top of his. He brought her hand to his lips and kissed it. "What's wrong?" he asked.

"Nothing. Just wishing my family had been as close as yours seems to be. But don't let that ruin this meal."

"If you ever want to talk about it, know that I'm here." He stroked her cheek and smiled.

"Thanks. This isn't something that I've talked about much. It just seemed like most of the people I hung out with didn't have strong family ties, and hearing about your family just makes me wonder if we could've and should've been closer."

"Every family is different. If Gran hadn't pulled us together when my mother was going through her stuff, there's no telling how I would've turned out."

Before their conversation could continue, Miss Lizzy walked out with a platter overflowing with food. Short ribs, pulled pork, coleslaw, potato salad, barbecue chicken and hush puppies.

"Give me a second and I'll be right back with a big pitcher of sweet tea. Or as some people around here call it, sweet table wine."

"Miss Lizzy, you have outdone yourself."

"Ooh, I forgot the mac and cheese." She slapped her hands against her thighs. "I'll bring that with the tea."

"Do you think we're going to eat all of this?"

Jamal nodded and took a rib from the platter. "Yes."

MJ grabbed a chicken wing and took a bite. She moaned in delight. "This is good."

"Told you." He held out a hush puppy to her. "This is better than mine, but don't go broadcasting that."

MJ bit into the hush puppy. "Your secret is safe with me. But this is delicious."

Miss Lizzy returned with the mac and cheese and tea. "Enjoy, guys."

About two hours later, MJ and Jamal sat at the table filled with empty plates, stuffed and satisfied.

"Whoo!" Jamal wiped his mouth. "That was amazing."

"I don't think I can eat another bite."

Miss Lizzy returned to the table with two small bowls of banana pudding. "Now, you can't leave without this."

Jamal smiled. "She's right. This banana pudding is the business."

"And I packed it to go, because y'all ate like you haven't had a meal in two weeks."

"You put your foot in this food, Miss Lizzy," Jamal said and Michael nodded in agreement.

"Well, thank you." Miss Lizzy turned to Michael. "You don't have to wait for this guy to bring you back here."

"I won't. This is a great spot. I can't wait to bring Mimi out here."

Jamal paid the bill and they headed to the car. He held his hand out for his keys, but MJ rolled her eyes and got into the driver's seat.

"But I thought this was part of the bet? How is it that you get to drive right now?"

"Because I drove here, it's only right that I drive back to my office."

"Woman logic. I understand."

"That's not sexist at all." Michael started the car. They rode in a comfortable silence, and then Michael put the mix CD in.

"This is dope." Jamal swayed to the music. "Who's the artist?"

"It's a mix of the artists who will be performing at the jazz fest. The CDs will be available at the clubs participating in the event."

"So many people will hear this and buy tickets. I almost want to get four right now."

"We're going to have to switch back to business mode when we get back to the office because we have the sites for the shows in place and I want you to go out there and outline what we need to do to keep people safe."

"I was wondering when you guys were going to get around to that."

MJ smiled. "Well, we finally got our act together."

Chapter 12

Michael was in awe as Jamal drew and wrote on the maps of each venue. Not that she'd had any doubts about his skill, but he obviously knew what he was doing. She was happy that she'd chosen his group to protect the jazz festival. Michael knew this could be a career-making event for her business. Despite all of the nonsense that had gone on in the planning of the festival, its success would make her one of the best marketing companies in Atlanta. Hell, the country.

"That smile is making me hot."

Michael focused on Jamal. "Can I tell you how much I appreciate you?"

"I'd rather you show me." He wiggled his eyebrows at her. "I know this event is important to you and I'm here to make sure there are no incidents that could mar it for you. So, anything I can do to make this successful, I'm all for it."

Michael crossed over to him and wrapped her arms around him. "You don't know what that means to me."

He brushed his lips against hers. "To your empire." Jamal captured her lips in a hot kiss that shook her soul. He was the kind of man she should've always wanted to have in her life. Someone who supported her dreams, looked out for what she was trying to establish for herself and not just what she could do for him. This was what love should feel like. This was the man she could build a future with. Right?

Jamal pulled back from her and smiled. "Don't think that amazing kiss changes the fact that I'm taking you down in the gym tonight."

"I almost want to let you win, but the fighter in me won't let me do that. Six thirty, right?"

"You got it." Jamal gave her a quick kiss on the lips. "So, if I'm going to be on time, I'd better go and take a look at these locations to see if I can implement these security plans."

"All right," she said. "See you tonight and I'm going to kick your ass at the gym."

"So you say." Jamal grinned then headed out the door.

Michael watched him leave and couldn't take her eyes off his tight bottom. She wondered if he wore gray sweatpants in the gym or tight shorts that hugged his muscles like a second skin. Either way, she couldn't wait to see it in a few hours. "'Bye, Jamal."

He turned around and smiled at her. "Don't be late for your beatdown."

* * *

Jamal headed for his car humming one of the jazz songs from the CD as he walked. When he felt a hand on his shoulder, he expected it to be Michael. But turning around, he saw that it was Lucy. *Shit*.

"Jamal, what's going on?"

"Why are you still stalking me?"

Lucy scoffed. "Okay, I'm not stalking you. I'm working with Michael on the jazz festival and we have a meeting. It's just a chance meeting."

"Sure it is. Lucy, what's your game?"

"Are you and Michael seeing each other?"

"How is that any business of yours?"

"Then I guess that is a yes. Wow. It makes sense why Nic said we should create a fan club for you. And I thought he was just jealous because he had competition. You know they have something hot."

"Had."

Lucy pulled out her phone and showed him a picture of MJ and Nic wrapped in each other's arms. Jamal kept his face neutral, but inside he was boiling with anger. Was she still seeing this guy? The asshole whom she claimed she was over? And of all people to see them together, it had to be Lucy?

"Nice," Jamal said.

"So, you're all right with this?"

"Goodbye, Lucy." He strode off from her and headed for his car.

"Jamal, you were all that I needed. All."

Ignoring her, he got into his car and zoomed out of

the parking lot. The aching thud in his chest must have been what it felt like to be heartbroken.

Michael ended her day with a smile on her face. She couldn't wait to see Jamal at the gym. Changing into her workout clothes, she sent him a text.

It's about to go down.

She headed downstairs to her car and drove to the gym, not paying attention to the fact that she hadn't gotten a response from him. When she arrived at the gym, Michael looked around the parking lot for Jamal's Mustang. When she didn't see it, she figured that she'd take advantage of her head start and warm up. After running on the treadmill for half an hour, she began to worry. Had Jamal been in an accident? She slowed her gait. Had something happened at work? Did she miss a text from him? She stopped the machine and pulled her phone from the back pocket of her yoga pants and dialed Jamal.

Voice mail.

Okay. What in hell is going on? Michael called him again. Still voice mail. She dashed out of the gym and sped to his house. As she drove, her mind was racing with the worst-case scenario. Had he been hurt? Did he need her?

Tears welled up in her eyes as she dialed his number again, fearing the worst.

Voice mail.

Jamal had ignored every call from MJ as he sat at the bar downing shot after shot of Fireball Whisky. How could she do this to him, then turn around and smile in his face? This was a game that he'd never played. Now he'd been played. Jamal tapped the bar for another shot. Part of him wanted to head over to Nic's jazz spot and punch him in the face. Then he'd send MJ a picture of her lover. But that would make him look like the jerk. The jerk in this situation was Michael.

His phone rang again. He looked at Michael's smiling face and wanted to toss the phone across the room. But still, he didn't answer. The bartender set another glass of whiskey in front of him. Jamal downed it and turned his back to the bar. When he saw Lucy coming his way, he wished he'd been able to move faster so that he could get away from her.

"Jamal, I thought that was your car outside. How are you doing?" she said as she took a seat beside him.

"What do you want?" He felt the need for another drink.

"Rude."

"I want to be alone."

"And get drunk? What's going on with you?"

Jamal glared at her but kept silent. That didn't keep Lucy from running off at the mouth, though.

"Jamal, I told you that we would be so good together. There is no one in Atlanta that understands you the way I do."

"Please. Stop."

She inched closer to him. "Just give us a chance."

"No. Lucy, let it go. We had one date. It wasn't a good one. You built this fantasy in your head about us being in a relationship, having a relationship or developing a relationship. It's not going to happen. It was never going to happen. So, stop following me around, thinking that I'm going to settle for you."

"At least I would've been faithful. I wouldn't be entertaining another man in my office under the guise of working together. You're going to get what you deserve. The heartbreaker's heart gets broken. Karma actually works." Lucy rose to her feet and stormed out of the bar.

Jamal gritted his teeth. Was he being foolish because he was taking a picture that Loony Lu-Lu showed him as the truth?

Still, he'd had doubts about the real deal with Nic and MJ anyway. The way she'd talked about wanting a family and hoped to have one by now. He had no doubt that she was talking about Nic. Maybe working on this festival was reviving her feelings for him.

Dropping money on the bar, he headed out to his car. When he saw the slashed front tires and cracked windshield, he didn't have to wonder who did it.

"Damn it!" He called AAA to tow the car away, and then he dialed Brent.

"What's up, man? You and Michael came up for air?"

"I need a favor. Can you come pick me up?"

"What's going on?" Brent's voice took on a serious timbre.

Jamal told him about the picture that Lucy had shown him of MJ and Nic embracing in her office and how he'd come to the bar to drown his sorrow in whiskey. Then he recounted how Lucy had shown up and pleaded for the two of them to be together.

"She has gone off the deep end." Brent sighed. "How long has she been stalking you?"

"Who knows? Then I come out to my car and the windshield is smashed and two tires are slashed. The worst thing about all of this is that she's the one who caught MJ with the guy she said she wanted nothing to do with. MJ had said she and Nic were over."

"Ask yourself this—how do you know that picture wasn't photoshopped or that it was a moment that didn't mean anything? Have you talked to Michael?"

"No."

"That's mature."

"Are you coming to get me or do I need to call Uber?"

"On my way. But do me a favor. Fix your attitude before I get there."

Jamal hung up the phone and walked back into the bar. He needed another drink.

Michael was frantic with worry. She paced back and forth in Jamal's driveway. Had he gotten in an accident because of his need for speed in that car? Instead of calling him again, she called Mimi.

"Girl, what's going on?"

"I think something has happened to Jamal. We were supposed to meet two hours ago. He's not answering the phone and he's not at home. Oh, my God, Mimi, I'm so scared."

"Okay, okay, calm down. I'm going to call Brent on three-way and see if he's heard from him."

"Yes, yes, please do that." Michael's hands shook as she waited for Mimi to come back on the line.

"Mimi, calm down. I'm going to pick Jamal up right now." Michael sighed when she heard Brent say that.

"Where is he?" Michael asked.

"Mimi, you got me on three-way?"

"Brent, she was worried."

"Hello!" Michael interjected. "Where is Jamal?"

"He's sitting at a bar. I'm going to pick him up and take him home."

Michael rubbed her forehead. "A bar? He's at a damned bar? I thought he was in a ditch dead and he's drinking at a bar."

"Michael," Brent said. "Calm down. You two need to talk. Why don't you wait for him at his place?"

"Obviously his phone is working because he called you. Do you know how many calls and texts I sent this man? He can talk to the stars, because I'm out."

"Michael, give him a chance to explain himself," Mimi said. "You…"

Michael hung up the phone and hopped in her car. Speeding out of the driveway, she drove to the gym because she needed to punch something, preferably Jamal's face.

Heading for the heavy bag, she picked up a pair of gloves and started punching. An hour later, she was covered in sweat, sore and pissed. If Jamal had been in the bar all of this time, why didn't he answer the phone? Why didn't he respond to her text messages? Snatching her gloves off, she stalked over to the drink machine and bought a liter of water. She downed it in three gulps, but the cold water didn't calm the burning anger inside her. This was the reason she hadn't wanted to open up to Jamal, share her feelings with him and fall in love with him. But she did, and once again, her heart had been smashed in thousands of pieces. Never again.

Michael headed for the shower and drowned her tears in the cold water. She was tired. Tired of believing that she would've been happy with Jamal. Right now, she didn't even care what his excuse was for not showing up or taking her calls. She just wanted to finish working on this jazz festival and get out of his life.

When she made it home, Michael turned off her phone and climbed into bed. Sleep would be her best friend tonight.

Brent pulled into Jamal's driveway and glanced at his friend. "You good over there?"

"Yeah. So, you talked to MJ?"

Brent nodded. "She called Mimi because she was worried about you. Then she got upset. You two need to talk and work this thing out. At the end of the day, you still have to work with her on the jazz fest."

"I have other people who can handle that."

Brent shook his head. "I know you care about this woman, so you need to stop acting like a spoiled asshole."

"And if you'd seen a picture of Mimi hugged up with her ex, you would've been all right with that? If I'm not mistaken, you were willing to leave her because of a blog post."

"This has nothing to do with me. My issue with

Mimi dealt more with the legal ramifications of people thinking that I was sleeping with my client. You know, the same thing my father did that landed him in prison."

Jamal ran his hand across his face. "So, I'm out here acting like a fool?"

"You said it."

Jamal reached into his pocket and dialed MJ's number. It went straight to voice mail. "I guess she's playing my game now."

"Can you blame her? She called you for hours and you ignored her."

"Well…"

"And you should've given her a chance to explain. Keep in mind you've dated half of the women in Atlanta. She's watched broads throw drinks in your face and yet gave you the benefit of the doubt. You see one picture and flip out. A picture from a woman who you know would do anything to ruin your life."

"Okay, okay, I messed up. I got to give her a chance to explain, but that was her office. Who knows what happened before Lucy showed up."

Brent slapped his hand on his forehead as he put the car in Park. "For the last time, I'm telling you that you've lost your mind. Maybe you wanted this to happen because you're too afraid to fall in love."

Jamal leaned back in his seat, not wanting to admit that his friend was right. But he was. He wanted to give MJ everything and that picture of her and Nic just made his soul ache.

"I'm going inside. Thanks for bringing me home."

"Truth hurts, huh?"

to be there for you every step of the way. Then you have me, who will be there for you when you drive him crazy."

Mimi sighed. "And that's why I'm going to move back to Atlanta full-time."

"Really? I know New Orleans was your dream."

"Being Mrs. Daniels is a much better dream. Besides, after the first termite swarm, I was kind of over New Orleans."

Michael laughed. "Welcome home, Mimi Collins."

"Where are we going?" Jamal asked as he snapped his seat belt in place.

"Breakfast. I have some big news for you." Brent started his car.

"Hopefully it doesn't come with a side of fireworks. My head is killing me."

"Overdid it last night, huh?"

Jamal sighed. "Ended up sleeping outside like a dope."

"Have you called Michael?"

"Nope. I know she doesn't want to talk to me, so I'm not wasting my time today."

Brent shook his head. "You need to talk to her, because she needs to explain that picture and the two of you are going to be spending a lot of time together."

"Not really."

"Yes, you are. Who do you think is going to be my son's godmother?"

"Son? You actually knocked Mimi up. Congrats, bruh! So, we're having a little raging Cajun?"

into his arms. "Michael, I'm sorry and I'm not going anywhere until you tell me that you forgive me."

"I'm going to need a little time for that." He could feel her anger wavering and he was going to take full advantage of it. Leaning in, Jamal captured her mouth in a slow kiss. She pressed her hand against his chest as if she was trying to push him away. But in a swift moment, she melted in his arms. When they broke the kiss, they stared into each other's eyes.

Jamal ran his index finger down the side of her cheek. "I'm sorry. And if you still need time, I'll give you that."

"I think I've had enough time. Can we make a promise right now?"

"What's that?"

"That we won't spend another night like last night?"

"That's a promise." Jamal kissed her forehead. "And we need to have an extended makeup session." He glanced over her shoulder and looked over at Mimi and Brent. "Without an audience."

"Guess that is our cue to leave," Brent said.

"Nope," Mimi countered. "I still have omelet on my plate."

MJ shook her head. "Why don't I just cook everybody some breakfast?"

Jamal wrapped his arm around her waist. "I'll help."

"Don't be in there getting nasty on the stove top!"

"Shut up, Mimi." Michael tossed a tangerine at her friend.

Alone in the kitchen, MJ and Jamal made quick work

of whisking the eggs and making two perfect omelets. "Please tell me you have Dancing Goat."

She shook her head. "But Mimi was kind enough to bring me some this morning. Pity you didn't pick up the phone last night."

"How long am I going to wear that?"

She shrugged as she plated the omelets. "Until I get tired of rubbing your nose in it. I mean, you robbed me of my victory at the gym last night."

"I did, but I got a clear morning. We can go ahead and end this right now."

"Let's eat and then we can go get it on."

Walking into the dining room, MJ set the plates on the table and Jamal gave her bottom a squeeze before taking his seat.

Mimi polished off the last of her omelet and smiled. "Babe, looks like our work here is done."

"Ambush reunion. That would be a great reality show."

Jamal shook his head. "Y'all are two of the corniest people I know. MJ, we're going to have to help baby boy Daniels grow up cool."

"You mean little Mimi? She's going to have a girl."

Brent and Mimi exchanged glances. "Maybe we'll have twins." Mimi stuck her fork in Brent's plate and took a piece of his eggs.

"You sure are eating like we are."

She threw her hand up at him. "This is just the beginning."

Jamal glanced over at MJ, remembering their careless night. He couldn't believe that he wanted this. He wanted her sneaking food off his plate, asking for a foot rub and carrying his child. And he'd been stupid enough to almost let it slip away because of Lucy and that picture.

"You don't want your omelet?" Mimi asked Jamal.

"Stay out of my plate. I'm not your husband. I don't have to share." He took a big bite of the omelet.

After breakfast, Mimi and Brent headed home and Jamal cleaned the kitchen while MJ got dressed for the gym. "Hey, MJ. I need to swing by my house and grab my gym bag. Since my ride left, do you mind taking me?"

She bounded down the stairs. "Sure. We can even go to the gym in your neighborhood. That way you can clean out your car and get it ready for me."

He placed his hands on her shoulders. "About my car. Sally is in the hospital."

"Really? What happened?"

"Someone must have been jealous of her beauty. Windshield smashed and a couple of tires slashed."

MJ raised her eyebrow but didn't say anything.

"What?" he asked.

"That sounds like a scorned woman type of thing."

Jamal knew she was right, but he was not ready to get into that conversation right now. He figured that Lucy had damaged his car, but he knew the dive bar probably didn't have security cameras that would show her in the act. "I'm going to write it off as a minivan driver who was just really mad about the current state of his or her vehicle."

"Whatever. Or you did it yourself because you're about to get your butt kicked by a girl." She flexed her muscles and then bounced out the door. Jamal stayed a few steps back so that he could get a full view of her amazing ass.

Michael glanced over at Jamal as she drove. Could they make it? Were they going to be able to put distrust of old relationships behind them and move forward together? Lord knew she'd tried. And Jamal hadn't given her a reason not to believe him.

"What's up?" he asked.

"Just thinking. You know, this wasn't supposed to happen."

He nodded. "Mimi told me to leave you alone."

"Thank you for not listening."

"I knew I had you when you tasted my hush puppies."

"And at some point in this forgiveness thing, you need to whip up a batch for me."

Jamal winked. "Gladly. As a matter of fact, we can have some for lunch. That is if you're still talking to me after you lose this burpee challenge."

Michael rolled her eyes as she pulled into Jamal's driveway. "Whatever."

They headed inside and Jamal dashed into his bedroom, while Michael looked around the living room. Then she crossed over to the sunroom and smiled. The night they'd spent there had been beautiful and so romantic. She almost wanted to pretend that he won the gym challenge and just make love to him on oversize pillows while the sun beat down on them.

Chapter 14

Over the next month and a half, Jamal and Michael were basically joined at the hip. They spent their mornings working on the security plans for the upcoming jazz festival and their nights making love. What Michael loved most about being with him was how he made her laugh and how he was such a tender lover.

The more time they spent together, the more she wanted to tell him how much she loved him. But something always stopped her. Whether it was a ringing cell phone or a client showing up out of the blue. Then there were the quiet moments when they were alone and doubt set in.

Just like right now. His lips brushed against her neck and Michael's eyes fluttered open. "Did I wake you?"

"Yes, but you knew you would." Michael looked up

even though she'd had breakfast with Jamal. She had a feeling that she was going to need a lot of energy for the day, especially if she was going to have to deal with Lucy this afternoon. Part of her wondered what Jamal had ever seen in the other woman apart from her pretty face. Then again, he did say that they'd gone out only once.

That must have been a hell of a date.

Jamal walked into his office and told his assistant to hold his calls for a half hour. He was tired of Lucy and now he could actually call it stalking. Sighing, he kept the lights off in his office, and when his cell phone rang, he almost yelled at his assistant, until he realized it wasn't his office phone.

"Yeah?"

"Jamal, this is Harry. I know I was supposed to get back with you a few weeks ago, but things have been a little hectic for me."

"It's good to hear from you, man."

"You might not say that after what I have to tell you."

"You're not coming back to First Line of Defense?"

"Nope. I'm going to retire and head down to Florida. However, you better be careful and watch your back."

"What do you mean?"

"Jamal, you got a crazy lady on your hands and trust me about that. I passed by your place a few nights ago and I saw she was staking out your place as if she was Atlanta Police."

"Really?"

"Yeah, and I'm sorry that I haven't gotten around to telling you sooner. Lucy acts as if she is classy and has a lot going for herself, but I've heard some stories."

"I don't think I want to know. But hey, man, thanks for calling and I appreciate the warning."

"No problem. Now, if you need anything, give me a call and I got you."

"Thanks, man!" After hanging up the phone, Jamal realized that his break was over. Turning the lights on in his office, he was ready to get to work and push Lucy out of his mind. But he was definitely going to get a security camera set up around his house.

After going through some requests for security, Jamal looked down at his watch and saw that it was about time to meet with MJ. He'd found a flaw in their security plan that they needed to get taken care of before the event. Jamal threw a dart at the calendar on his wall. Two more weeks of this and then he wouldn't have to deal with these crazy club owners anymore.

The threat of Hurricane Dylan forced the Carver low-country boil to be postponed and Gran decided to make it this year's Thanksgiving celebration. Jamal had been happy because he hadn't had a chance to get fresh crawfish with all of the craziness going on.

He couldn't help but think about what Harry had said. Was Lucy dangerous or just a spoiled brat trying to get her way? He shook those thoughts away and headed for his car. Right now, he was going to focus on getting security tight for the jazz festival. He didn't want anything to mar the event. The right people were watching and he wanted MJ to get all the credit she deserved for putting on a great show.

Michael smiled when noon rolled in and Lucy hadn't shown up in her office. She buzzed her assistant.

"Yes, Miss Jane?"

"If Lucy Becker shows up, please let her know that I'm in a meeting."

"Yes, ma'am. Mr. Carver just walked in. Are you available?"

Michael smiled. "Of course."

"I'll send him in."

She smoothed her skirt and wiped her mouth before he walked in.

Jamal smiled as he crossed the threshold. "Hello, beautiful. Sorry to stop by unannounced."

Michael crossed over to him and gave him a tight hug. "Stop by anytime. What's going on?"

He pointed to her desk. "Let's have a seat. I was going over the security plan and I saw a few soft spots." Jamal rolled out the blueprints of all of the outdoor venues where concerts were scheduled and pointed out the flaws.

"How do we fix that?"

"Easy fix is a gate. Best plan, I think, is a gate and two more people back there. This is where local law enforcement will come in handy. I have all hands on deck and I don't have another man or woman that I can put back there."

Michael nodded. "If you think having additional officers will keep everyone safe, then that's what we will have to do."

"MJ, I want you to win. Because when this goes well, the city of Atlanta is going to know the marketing genius you are and they are going to beat a path to your front door."

"From your mouth to God's ear."

Jamal walked over to Michael's seat and stood in front of her. With a big smile on his face, he leaned into her—their foreheads pressed against each other's—and brushed his lips against hers. "I see big things in your future. And a big kiss."

"Let me have it."

Jamal captured her lips, nibbling her bottom lip, sucking her tongue and making her moan. She wrapped her arms around his neck, pulling him closer. Jamal's body felt so good. His kiss heated her like a desert afternoon. As his hand slipped between her thighs, Michael knew she wasn't going to get any work done until she had a chance to feel him deep inside her.

"MJ. I've always wondered how comfortable your desk is." Jamal swiped the papers on her desk onto the floor. "Shall we find out?"

"Yes." Her voice was a husky whisper as Jamal lifted her from her seat and laid her on the desk. Hiking her skirt up, he dropped to his knees and pulled her panties down. Spreading her thighs apart, he buried his face between them, lapping and sucking her sweetness. Michael gripped his head as she moaned in pleasure. She pressed her body deeper into his kiss.

"Yes, yes! That feels so good."

Jamal continued pleasuring her, slipping his hands underneath her shirt and tweaking her diamond-hard nipples. Michael's body burned with need as his tongue made circles around her clitoris. Her desire wet his face as she exploded. "Jamal!"

Pulling back from her, he smiled at the sated look on her face. "Oh, we're not done. That was just part one of the desktop fantasy." Winking at her, Jamal dropped his pants to his ankles. She reached down and stroked his hardness. Then she pushed him back in her desk chair. "Was this a part of the fantasy as well?" Michael eased down his body and took the length of him into her mouth. Suck. Lick. Suck.

Jamal groaned as her tongue grazed the tip of his throbbing penis. She felt his shiver as she licked him like the sweet chocolate he was.

"Ooh, ride me, baby. I need to be inside you now."

She mounted him, guiding him inside and reveling in the way he felt as he filled her with desire and pleasure. Grinding and sliding in the chair, Michael and Jamal bumped and ground against each other until they both exploded. She leaned against his chest, trying to catch her breath.

"Did it end like that?"

Jamal shook his head. "But this is one time when I'm happy to say reality outweighed my fantasy." He kissed her gently on the cheek. "We need some food to regain all the energy we just expended, since we still have work to do."

"But we're the bosses, right? Why don't we take the rest of the day off and have lunch in bed?"

"That's the best idea I've heard all day. My place or yours?"

"My bed is closer." She winked at him as they fixed their clothes and got ready to leave the office.

Chapter 15

Jamal almost beat MJ to her house. He was so looking forward to spending the rest of the day wrapped in her arms. But when he and MJ arrived at her place, he was shocked to see Lucy there.

"My God," he muttered as he parked his car and got out. The look on MJ's face said she was just as appalled as he was.

Lucy clasped her hands together. "I'm glad both of you are here."

"What are you doing at my house—again?" MJ shook her head in disgust. "We've already had this conversation."

"I know, and I was going to come by your office, but that seemed so indelicate. This is a private matter that I thought we should talk about in private. It's just an added bonus that he's here."

Jamal stood between the two women. "Lucy, you have to stop this."

"Jamal, you're the cause of this!"

He furrowed his brows at her. "What are you talking about?"

"Tell her about the other night."

MJ looked from Lucy to Jamal. "What is she talking about?"

Lucy folded her arms across her chest and tilted her head to the side. "Jamal, you need to come clean. You need to tell her the truth."

Jamal squeezed his forehead. "You're not making any sense."

Lucy pulled her phone from her purse. "This! When are you going to stop acting as if we're not together when we spent the night just a few days ago." She flashed the picture of her draped across Jamal's sleeping body. MJ snatched the phone from her hand and studied the photo.

"This is your backyard, Jamal."

"This didn't happen."

MJ slapped him. "Don't stand here and lie to me. This. Is. Your. Backyard. Your special place that you don't share with anyone."

"I'm sorry you had to find out this way," Lucy interjected. "But Jamal plays these games, toys with women and always comes out looking like a rose."

"How about both of you get the hell off my property!"

"MJ, you can't…"

She threw her hand up in his face. "Don't you say a word to me, you lying bastard."

"MJ, please! You can't…"

"Control what I'm going to do if you don't get out of my face!"

As MJ turned on her heels and slammed inside her house, Jamal crossed over to Lucy and glared at her. "What in the hell kind of game are you playing? You know damn well that nothing has ever happened between us."

"Well, a picture is worth a thousand words, and she believed every one of them. I told you that one day you'd pay for playing with all of these women as if they were pawns on a chessboard. Here is your reckoning." Lucy smiled coldly at him. If Jamal had been a lesser man, he would've stuffed her in his trunk and dropped her off in Lake Lanier. Instead, he bounded toward MJ's door. He wasn't going to leave until she heard him out.

Michael ignored the doorbell for five minutes, because she'd been crying her eyes out and Jamal didn't deserve her tears.

After five more minutes, she was tired of hearing the damn ringing. Why hadn't he left when she told him to? How could he explain that woman lying in his arms in what was supposed to be their special place? He'd been the one who said he didn't take women back there. He'd made her feel special when he showed her the stars and his softer side. Jamal had been so sweet, tender and loving. He'd made her believe that the playboy Jamal Carver had died and he was all hers.

Liar! She'd made a fool of herself again and she was tired of being a fool for love. And she loved him. She loved Jamal more than she had been willing to admit. And once again, she'd found herself on the wrong side of heartbreak.

Another ring. Was he insane? One thing was for sure: Jamal wasn't going to leave and Michael couldn't stand that damned doorbell anymore. She crossed over to the door and snatched it open.

"What part of 'get the hell off my property' don't you understand?"

"MJ, I'm not leaving until you hear me out."

She pushed him against his chest. "What can you say? She was in your backyard, on that precious patio that you never took a woman to until me, right?" She pushed him again. "I don't know why I fell for your lies when I knew you were a snake."

"Really?"

She narrowed her eyes at him, but Michael knew she was being harsh. "I knew you weren't a one-woman man, but I trusted you and you broke that and my heart."

"You can't take her word over mine without giving me a chance to…"

"I'm not taking anyone's word. I saw the picture. She was in our space, in your arms! What's supposed to be the takeaway from that? Jamal, please just go!" Michael felt her eyes burning with unshed tears and she was not going to give him the satisfaction of seeing her cry.

"I'm going to go for now, but I'm not going to give up on us and you're going to see that I was never unfaithful to you. And for the record, we've been down this road with Lucy before. Is it just different now because you keep expecting me to hurt you?"

"Again. She was in our space. A woman who went on one date with a man isn't going to do all of this! Don't expect me to continue to buy the bullshit."

Michael walked over to the door and opened it. She didn't say a word as Jamal walked out. But when he left, she crumpled to the floor and sobbed.

Jamal left MJ's and drove around the city like a lost tourist. He tried to wrap his mind around how Lucy had gotten that picture. Yes, she was in his backyard and he was sleeping, but… The night came back to him a rush of memories that he'd written off as a dream. A few months ago, when he'd gone to sleep in his backyard after getting a little too tipsy at the bar, he'd felt something against him on the lounge chair. But between him being tired and drunk, he hadn't been able to open his eyes to see what was going on.

The next morning, he'd awakened to the chirping of birds and his sprinkler system spraying him in the face. But other than an extraordinary headache and wet pants, he didn't remember anything else. And he certainly didn't remember being with Lucy that night. How was he going to convince MJ of that?

Jamal wanted to turn around and go back to MJ's place and make her understand that he hadn't hurt her and he wasn't the guy she thought he was. Still, Lucy needed to be put in her place. He knew if he went to the police, he'd get laughed out of the station house. She may have been responsible for vandalizing his car, but there was no proof. She'd taken a picture at his house, but she hadn't broken any laws because he didn't have a No Trespassing sign on his property. He felt as if this woman was holding him prisoner. Jamal pulled out his cell phone and called Brent. Maybe his friend had some idea as to how he could help him.

Mimi shook her head as she shoveled a forkful of chocolate cake in her mouth. "I really thought he'd changed his ways. I was rooting for you guys and even started looking at maternity bridesmaid dresses." She let out a groan and then looked at Michael, who seemed to be on the verge of tears again. "I'm sorry."

"Not as sorry as I am. And that crazy bi... She came to my house, Mimi, twice!"

"She better be grateful that we aren't the M&M of ten years ago. She would be in a world of trouble."

"He isn't even worth dumping five pounds of sugar in her gas tank for." Michael swiped a piece of Mimi's cake. Popping it in her mouth, she tried to tell herself that if she stayed mad that she would hurt less.

Mimi licked her fork. "He is worth it and that's why you're hurting. I thought he'd changed, the way he'd call Brent and... Oops. I'm supposed to be minding my business."

"He'd call Brent and what?"

"Nothing."

Michael snatched Mimi's cake away. "MJ! You can't do this to your godchild."

"He'd call Brent and what?"

"From what I overheard, Jamal was falling hard and

fast for you. That's why something about this seems fishy."

"Mimi, there was a picture. She was all laid up on him in his backyard. Our spot." Michael handed Mimi her plate back then rose to her feet. She was glad her friend had kept her old place in Atlanta. Today, she needed a hiding spot, though Jamal could easily find her since Brent and Mimi did live across the hall in the condo complex. And as much as she wanted to pull up stakes and get out of town, she still had the jazz festival to promote. Looking out of the massive windows, Michael sighed. She had only a day, at the most, to avoid Jamal.

Damn.

"Mimi, are you in here?" Brent asked, causing Michael to turn around. Clearly, she didn't have a day to avoid Jamal because there he was with Brent.

"I'm leaving." Michael walked over to the sofa where Mimi sat, to grab her purse.

"Hear me out before you leave." Jamal stood in front of her, blocking her exit.

"What? What could you possibly have to say?"

"Can we talk alone?"

She shook her head. "I'm not going anywhere with you and I'm really not interested in what you have to say."

"So, I'm just supposed to let go because you said so?"

She turned her back to him and made the mistake of looking at Mimi and Brent. They'd been sitting on the sofa, Brent's arms around Mimi's shoulders and Mimi's head against his chest. For a brief second, she saw her and Jamal in that pose, remembered how happy she'd been in his arms as they looked at the stars. Was she willing to throw that away without giving him a chance to explain?

Was she willing to trust her heart not to get broken again?

"MJ? I just want the same chance I gave you."

She turned around and looked at him. "We have to work together for these next couple of weeks. But I don't have to move beyond that with you."

"You don't have to do anything you don't want to do, but you and I know that we're not over."

She ran her hand across her face, hating that he could see right through her. "If nothing happened between you two, then why did you invite her over?"

Jamal took her face in his hands. "You've seen yourself—she shows up where she wants to show up. I thought about when that picture might have been taken. Remember the night I acted like an ass and thought you'd kissed Nic?"

She nodded.

"I slept outside because I'd had too much to drink that night. Even in the picture you could see I was out cold. MJ, you have to believe in me, believe in us. You're the only woman I want in my life, in my arms and in my bed."

Everything he said made sense and she wanted to trust that he was right. Just as she was about to reply, her cell phone went off. Nic.

She wasn't surprised that he was calling, being that the jazz festival was so close. "Yes, Nic?"

"Is there a reason you're not in your office? Come on, MJ. We got to make sure everything is…"

"Nic, you're not my only client, and I sent you an email about all of the questions you had and a copy of the new security plan. What more do you need?"

"Well, I had a few questions and some suggestions about the after-parties at my club. And there's been a push for more of the mix CDs and I forgot where we've already distributed them. Can I be honest?"

"That would be a first," she quipped as she held her finger up to Jamal.

"I'm scared. This is big and I couldn't have done it without you."

"All right, Nic. I'll meet with you in the morning."

"Thanks."

Smiling, she hung up and focused on Jamal. The look on his face told her he had a lot of questions and Michael wasn't inclined to explain herself at all. "I'm going home."

"MJ." He touched her arm. "Don't give up on us."

She didn't reply as she walked out the door.

Jamal took about two seconds to think before he rushed out the door after MJ left. "MJ! I'm not giving up and I'm not going to let you turn what we've been building into a business relationship. Nothing happened with me and Lucy."

She turned around and faced him. "Why can't you just give me time?"

"Because what I feel can't wait. Damn it, I've waited my whole life to find one woman I could love, and now that I've found you, I'm not going to let anyone or anything come between us."

"This isn't just about you! I'm in this, too, and I'm

not trying to get my heart broken! You're going to break my heart. Maybe you're not going to do it on purpose. Maybe this thing with Lucy is some crazy accident, but what about the next time and the next woman? I knew who you were when I started seeing you."

"You made me better, MJ. You made me see that you're all I want or need." He took her face in his hands. "Don't do this."

Tears filled her eyes and Jamal's heart broke. The last thing he'd wanted was to ever make her cry. He didn't want to hurt MJ and he'd felt as if he'd done just that.

"What am I supposed to do?"

"Trust me, MJ. Trust me. Love me and let me love you." He captured her lips in a slow kiss. Jamal felt her melt against his body, felt as if her resistance was floating away. Pulling back from her, Jamal pressed his forehead against hers. "MJ."

"Jamal, please."

"I know you love me."

"What?"

"Say it."

"No."

"Say it."

"I love you."

"Then you owe it to us to keep going and I won't take no for an answer."

She stroked his cheek. "I'm not going to say no again."

Chapter 16

With the jazz festival less than twenty-four hours away, Michael was amazingly calm. The shows had sold out and the weather was expected to be perfect. She hoped that everything would go off without a hitch.

Nic burst into her office, breaking into her thoughts. "We have a problem."

"Hello to you, too." She shook her head.

"I don't have time for niceties when one of our headliners just dropped out!" Nic plopped down in the chair in front of Michael's desk.

"Who was it?"

"The Pink Brass Band. Lucy called me and told me five minutes ago. She said you two can't work together anymore as well. What's going on with that?"

Michael typed the band's name into her computer

and looked for their manager's number. The Pink Brass Band was one of the hottest groups in the nation and a huge part of the marketing of the jazz festival. She didn't understand why their management hadn't called her.

She snatched up the receiver on her phone and pounded the number into the keypad.

"Clayton Matthews," a voice answered.

"Clayton, this is Michael Jane. I just got a disturbing message about the Pink Brass Band."

"You were on my list to call this morning because I wanted to know why you guys decided at the last minute to pull my girls. Lucy called about two hours ago and I was shocked."

Michael narrowed her eyes. This woman was playing a serious game that wasn't going to end well. "Clayton, I'm so sorry for this mix-up. Please tell me you all haven't booked anything else."

"We didn't have time. My next booking was going to be at the courthouse to sue you guys for breach of contract. We gave up some big shows to do this festival."

"You don't have to do that. We still need your girls. I'll upgrade your housing for this mix-up."

"Thanks, MJ. I should've known not to listen to that rambling crazy lady."

After hanging up the phone, she held up her finger to Nic and started calling all of the other acts to see if Lucy had tried this trick with them as well.

MJ knew that the success of this festival could make her career, just as it being an epic fail could ruin everything she'd worked so hard for.

About thirty minutes later, she'd confirmed that no one else had received a call from Lucy. The entire time she'd been on the phone, Nic looked as if he was about to lose his lunch. If this hadn't been so important, she would've gotten glee from the torturous look on Nic's face. But this wasn't a game. Finally, MJ could put Nic's mind at ease. "Crisis averted, but why is Lucy trying to ruin this event?"

"I told you she was off in the head. But you insisted on working with her." Nic shook his head.

Michael closed her eyes and squeezed the bridge of her nose. "Listen, we don't have to talk about shoulda, woulda, coulda. We have to make sure this festival goes off without a hitch. We've planned for months and we should have the greatest weekend ever in the jazz community."

"And then what's next for us?" Nic smiled.

"Nothing."

"You have to admit that we made a great team."

She laughed and shook her head. "Nic, we didn't make a great team. You were very difficult to work with and I wish I'd recognized this years ago. But this was a great idea." What she didn't tell him was how she'd already seen a bump in clients because of the branding of the jazz fest and her handling of the marketing.

She also didn't tell him about the drama with Lucy and Jamal. "Do you need anything else?" Michael rose to her feet and glanced at her watch. She was meeting Jamal for lunch and she needed to get going.

"I think we're done. You've done an amazing job and I'm glad we got a chance to work together on this."

She smiled. "It was interesting." She extended her hand to him and Nic laughed.

"This where we are now?"

Michael nodded. Nic pursed his lips. "Girl, give me a hug!" Nic enveloped Michael in his arms and gave her a tight, brotherly hug. "I know that we're not the friends we used to be, but you will always have a place in my heart."

"That's sweet. Nic, I wish you the best."

They headed out the door together and Michael felt as if the book was closed on her and Nic forever, business and personal.

Jamal shut down his computer. He was in need of a kiss from MJ because this jazz fest was getting on his nerves. Between the calls from the police and sheriff's departments about his security plans and watching his back to see if Lucy was lurking around, he was tired.

When his phone rang, he was tempted not to answer, but since it was Gran, he picked up.

"My queen."

"Don't 'my queen' me. I haven't heard from you in a couple of weeks."

"Sorry, Gran, I've been busy, and I know that's no excuse. But I still love you."

"I can't tell. Anyway, you have my crawfish ordered?"

Jamal hated to lie to his gran, but he hadn't ordered the crawfish. "I have."

"You've never been a good liar. If you bring frozen crawfish this year, I'm writing you out of my will."

"No frozen crawfish, not that I've ever brought you frozen crawfish anyway. Gran, I'm bringing someone with me."

"Really? Now, is she the special one you've been asking me questions about?"

"Yes, and MJ is the one."

"You better be sure, because the last thing that you should do is make that woman love you when you have no intentions to make a lasting future with her."

"I don't have a future without MJ."

He could feel the smile on Gran's face through the phone line. "Look who's grown up. I can't wait to meet this woman."

"You will and you're going to love her. I have to go, but I'm glad you called and you know that I love you more than the stars."

"Make sure you show me that love with fresh crawfish!"

After hanging up, Jamal heard the door open. MJ walked in with a huge smile on her face.

"Hey." She kicked her heels off.

"Hey, you." He crossed over to her and pulled her into his arms. "One more day."

"I know."

She sighed as they broke their embrace. Jamal took her face in his hands. "What's wrong?"

"Lucy Becker."

Jamal groaned. "Don't say her name. She might pop up like a ghost. What did she do?"

"Tried to cancel one of our headliners at the last minute. Nic came into my office this morning in a tizzy."

"Really? Did you get it handled?"

"Of course. I'm going to be so happy when this is over."

"Ready to head out for lunch?"

"Why don't we order in?" She smiled. "You're the only person I want to be around right now."

Jamal smiled then licked his lips. "I like the sound of that." He walked over to his computer and pulled up an online menu for his favorite Thai restaurant. Since he and MJ had Thai food at least once a week, he already knew what to order. "The food will be here in about thirty minutes." Jamal rose to his feet and turned the lights off. Then he sat down and motioned for MJ to sit on his lap.

"Thank you for believing in us."

"Thank you for giving me a reason to believe. Jamal, I love you."

"Love you more. You changed my life and I couldn't be happier."

She stroked his cheek. "Jamal."

In a quick swoop, he captured her full lips in a hot kiss. She melted against his chest as the kiss deepened. Jamal was thankful for that skirt she was wearing. His hands had free access to her thighs and that sweet spot between them.

MJ moaned as his thumbs brushed across her throbbing bud, making her body burn with desire. Just as he was about to slip her panties off, there was a knock at the door.

"Damn, just when I was ready to eat."

MJ eased off his lap and Jamal went to get their food.

* * *

While Jamal paid for their lunch, Michael received a Google alert on her phone. When she saw it was about Mimi's blog on the jazz fest, she couldn't wait to read it.

Atlanta is about to host the biggest music festival for jazz lovers. It's going to be chock-full of food, fun and great music. I had a chance to talk to the members of my new favorite band, Pink Brass Band. They're an all-female jazz band from Atlanta. All of their instruments are pink and they sound great! The creator of the band, Nadine Oakley, said she wanted to show the world that women could play real music and didn't have to trade on their bodies to be successful.

Now, make no mistake, these women are beautiful, but you won't see them dancing around the stage in leotards showing off their boobs and booty.

"We are much more than our looks. We write our music, we play our music and we look good doing it fully dressed."

They got the idea to be a brass band after a trip to New Orleans when they were college students. Seeing the music at the clubs and on the street made them want to bring part of that back to Atlanta.

"But we had to put our spin on it. When we painted our instruments pink, we gained a lot of attention. Then people listened to us and they were hooked."

They started headlining regional festivals, and three years ago, they signed a deal with one of the biggest jazz labels in the country. Then pink became the color of success. The group was nominated for a Grammy and have two platinum records under their belt.

Even with their critical success, there are people in the A who haven't heard the Pink Brass Band play. That all changes tomorrow when they take the main stage at the inaugural Atlanta Jazz Festival. Things get started at noon.

Log on to www.atlantajazzfest.org for a list of performance times and all of the food trucks that will be on the scene, including the amazing Sunshine Café's mobile restaurant.

"Good job, Mimi," she said as she set her phone on Jamal's desk.

Jamal crossed over to MJ. "Food. What are you smiling about?"

"Mimi's blog."

"Do I even want to know?"

"It's about the jazz fest." MJ playfully punched him on the shoulder. "That food smells delicious. Let's eat."

Licking his lips, Jamal smiled. "I know what I was trying to eat."

"So nasty." She smiled as Jamal pulled the food out of the bags.

They sat down and enjoyed pad Thai orange chicken and rice. After they finished eating, Jamal and MJ nestled on the love seat in the corner of his office and drifted off to sleep. And she didn't have to dream, because it had come true already.

Chapter 17

The morning of the jazz fest, the nerves finally hit Michael. She was praying that everything would go off without a hitch. Her duties were technically done, but she was connected to the event, and if anything went wrong she would be linked to it.

Sighing, she called Mimi again. Yes, it was early, yes, her best friend was pregnant, but today she needed a run.

"Hello?"

"Mimi, it's about time you answered."

"MJ, if you're not dying, I'm going to kill you."

"Can we go for a quick run and talk?"

Mimi exhaled into the phone. "Sure. The doctor said I should stay active and I haven't taken a run in two days. Can you do me a favor, though?"

"What?"

"Two chocolate doughnuts from Krispy Kreme. I've been craving one for two weeks and Brent won't get one for me."

"Why not? Because if your husband isn't on board with feeding you junk food, there is probably a good reason."

"He's mean and he claims that I should watch my sugar intake."

"I agree. So, I'll get you half a doughnut—only because I woke you up this morning."

"You're mean, too. I'll see you in fifteen minutes."

After hanging up with Mimi, Michael headed out to her balcony to get some fresh air. Smiling, she thought about Jamal and how he'd spent the night talking to her on the phone. It felt like being back in high school again.

She didn't notice that she was being watched from across the street.

Jamal and his security staff walked around the main stage area, making sure everything was set up properly for crowd control. It was early, but he wanted to make sure there were no glitches. Jamal was taking securing the jazz festival extra personal because he knew how important this was to MJ. She'd worked too hard for anything that he could prevent to go wrong.

"Have we gotten the reports from the metal detectors? They're online, right?"

"Yes, sir," Brad Stoops, the field commander, said. "We're waiting on the contractor to come in and put the fence up in the back of the park and then we're done."

"Great. I'm going to check the second location and then I need you guys to meet me at the office so that I can issue the vests."

"Got it."

As Jamal headed to his car, he pulled out his cell phone and called MJ.

"You're up early," she said when she answered.

"So are you. How are you feeling this morning?"

"Nervous, scared, excited."

"Well, I have some great news for you—security is tight."

She laughed and Jamal felt the warmness of her smile through the phone line. "I knew it would be. That's why I wanted First Line of Defense."

"And I thought it was just because you wanted me."

"I was going to have you anyway."

"Is that so?"

"Please, don't act like you would've said no."

Jamal laughed. "You're right. What are you doing right now?"

"Standing on the balcony, watching the sunrise and waiting for Mimi so that we can go on a run."

"I talked to Mimi yesterday. Is she trying to get you to get her chocolate doughnuts?"

"Yes. What's up with that?"

"Brent said the doctor told her she has to cut down on her caffeine intake. No chocolate and no coffee."

"She's not going to make it. Poor Mimi."

"Well, as her best friend and the future godmother of my godson, you need to make sure you keep her de-caffeinated."

"Will do." Jamal heard MJ's doorbell ring.

"I'd better go. I think Mimi is here."

"MJ, I love you. See you later."

"Love you, too."

After hanging up with his woman, Jamal was all smiles. He couldn't help thinking about Brent and Mimi, though. He wanted the life they were having, preparing to welcome a baby into the world. MJ in a white dress flashed before his eyes, and though he needed to check on security measures at the other venues, he wanted to go and look at engagement rings. Today was going to be the day that he asked MJ to marry him.

As soon as Michael opened the door, Mimi asked, "Where's my doughnut?"

Michael shook her head. "Not doing it. Jamal told me what the doctor said about chocolate and coffee. I have to protect my future goddaughter."

Mimi rolled her eyes. "Fine."

"But I do have something for you. A blueberry smoothie."

Mimi folded her arms across her chest. Michael laughed.

"If you close your eyes you can pretend that it's a chocolate milk shake." They headed into the kitchen.

"When I announce my pregnancy on the blog, I'm so telling this story."

"When are you going to do that? I've been waiting to see how your readers are going to react to the news. I'm still trying to wrap my mind around it myself." Michael dropped the blueberries and ice in the blender. "Almond milk or soy milk?"

"No dairy?"

"Nope."

"Soy. And Brent isn't exactly excited about our private life going public again. That's why I've been holding back. I get where he's coming from, but over the years, I feel like my blog has become more than just a place for me to rant. I share my joy and pain with my readers and this is the best thing that has ever happened to me and I want to share it with the world."

"This opens a whole new avenue for you and your blog. The Mis-Adventures of Motherhood."

Mimi reached out and hugged her friend. "You are a marketing genius. I'm so scared, MJ. I don't know if I'm ready to be a mom."

"Girl, you're going to be awesome. You have so much love to give and a great support system."

Tears welled up in Mimi's eyes. "I'm glad you're here for me. There are some things men don't get and I need you to listen."

"You know I got you. And we're going to drink these smoothies until you give birth."

Mimi looked at the purple juice in the blender. "Yeah, no."

Michael poured the smoothies in two glasses. "Drink."

They drank the smoothies and then headed out for their run. Instead of their normal three miles, they ran one mile in silence. Michael's mind was on the jazz festival and she silently prayed that nothing would go wrong over the next two days.

"Can we stop now?" Mimi asked.

"Yes! I was wondering if you were going to be super pregnant woman."

"So did I, but I see that I can't do it all." Mimi took a deep breath. "I think this is going to be my first blog post."

"I can't wait to read it and you better tell the whole truth."

Once they were back at Michael's, Mimi and her best friend settled down on the sofa and love seat then went to sleep.

The ringing of MJ's cell phone woke them up. "Hello?"

"Where are you, MJ?"

"Oh, Jamal, Mimi and I went to sleep. Give me about twenty minutes and I'll be at the park." Michael rose to her feet, and then she woke Mimi up.

"Everything is actually looking good around here. The food trucks are getting set up and it smells amazing."

"Have people started coming out yet?"

"There are a few hundred people here so far."

"Okay. Let me and Mimi get ready and we're on our way."

Mimi stretched her arms above her head. "I guess that nap was way too good."

Michael nodded. "I meant to get to the park around nine thirty, but sometimes you have to listen to your body."

Mimi picked up her keys and told MJ she'd see her at the park.

"Meet me by the main stage. Jamal said it's getting pretty crowded out there."

"Cool. I know Brent said that he'd come out after court this afternoon. I want to hit up the food trucks without his watchful eye on me."

"Umm, huh. You're still staying away from chocolate," Michael called out as she walked out the door.

MJ hopped in the shower and got dressed then sped to the park. Jamal met her at the entrance of the park and walked her through the metal detectors. "You look amazing," he said as he drank in her image in her white sundress and strappy sandals.

She spun around. "You like? Got to love Atlanta weather. It's October and still seventy degrees. I couldn't have ordered a better day from Mother Nature herself."

He nodded and took her into his arms. "I don't just like it—I love it. White looks good on you."

MJ looked around the park, happy to see the crowds growing. "This is really nice."

"You worked hard on this event. You should be proud." Jamal kissed her on the forehead.

"Thank you. I'm glad the work is over."

Jamal nodded as he watched people entering the park.

"I'm glad we ended up using the metal detectors," MJ said. "I feel a lot more comfortable with this given the state of the world."

Jamal nodded. "I can't believe we actually had an

argument about it. But that's neither here nor there. We get to have fun now."

Locking hands, Jamal and MJ headed toward the food truck staging area to check out the grub.

In the distance, Lucy watched the couple, her face showing how angry she was seeing them together. "What does she have that I don't?" she muttered as she followed them with her eyes. "I told him he was going to pay for playing with people's hearts and it's time for him to do just that."

As the music started, Jamal watched MJ's hips sway while she took a bite of a funnel cake corn dog. Those lips. His lips. He loved everything about this woman and he couldn't wait to ask her to be his wife. He hadn't gotten the ring he wanted for her, but the emerald-and-diamond ring in his pocket was the pre-engagement ring he was going to give her when he asked her to marry him later today. He wanted to take his fiancée to Savannah, not his girlfriend.

"What? Do I have powdered sugar on my face?" She locked eyes with him.

"No. I was just thinking that you should share." He laughed. MJ held her corn dog out to him and Jamal took a big bite. Huge mistake.

"My God, that is too sweet."

"That's what makes it great. However, I don't think I'd add this to my daily food choices. Like a wise man once told me, you have to try it to make sure you don't like it."

Jamal pointed to a pizza food truck. "I'm going to keep it safe and simple."

"Chicken."

They walked over to the food truck. After Jamal ordered his slice, MJ turned to him with a smile on her face.

"How many security guards do you have working today?"

"Between the two locations, I have about a hundred guards and then I have a crew that works the after-parties. Speaking of, are we going to hit up any of them?"

MJ shook her head furiously. "I don't want to be out when the sun goes down because I'm so over this."

Jamal kissed her cheek. "I'm so glad to hear you say that. Because tonight, I want to wrap you up in my arms and watch the stars."

"In the sunroom?"

"Yes. And we can make love all night long."

MJ moaned slightly. "Can we leave now?"

"That would be so irresponsible." He winked at her. "But I'm very tempted." Looking at MJ again in that white dress, he couldn't help but think about watching her walk down the aisle into his arms. Though the band on the stage was playing an up-tempo rendition of Stevie Wonder's "Ribbon in the Sky," all Jamal heard was the "Wedding March."

"Jamal? Are you okay?"

"Yeah, yeah, just thinking about your naked body and how irresponsible I want to be right now."

She pinched him on the shoulder. "Stop it."

Taking his pizza slice, Jamal and MJ moved toward the stage to listen to the music for a while.

"I love the sound of this band," MJ said, still moving to the beat. "I think they were on the CD compilation."

"They do sound great." Jamal tossed his pizza crust in a nearby trash can. "Let's dance." Taking her in his arms, Jamal spun Michael around as the band played. The people around them smiled as they watched their moves. Jamal dipped MJ twice and she broke into a salsa move that drew cheers from the crowd.

Once the song ended, Jamal and MJ drew as much applause as the band. "I need water," MJ said. "That was fun."

"It was." As they turned to head for one of the drink stations, they ran into Lucy.

"Well, isn't this cozy." She folded her arms across her chest.

"Lucy, please don't make a scene," Jamal said.

"A scene? I'm here for retribution!" Lucy reached into her purse and Jamal leaped into action. He tackled Lucy and a .22 caliber pistol spilled from her purse. MJ kicked it away as Jamal reached for his zip tie to secure Lucy's hands.

"You can't do this to me! You've played with hearts and you broke mine! I hate you!"

Jamal pressed the button on the radio on his shoulder to call for backup. Lucy looked up at MJ. "You're not special. He's going to toss you aside like trash soon enough."

"One date." Jamal gritted his teeth. "We went on one date and it didn't work out. Get over it, Lucy."

MJ backed away from them and released a sigh. She had no idea that Lucy was that insane. "How did she get a gun in here?" MJ watched as two Atlanta PD officers hauled Lucy off.

"I don't know, but I'm about to find out." Jamal took long strides to the entrance. He grabbed the guy manning the metal detectors. "How in hell did someone get in here with a gun?"

"Everyone has been going through the metal detectors. I don't know what happened."

The guard watched as Lucy was carted out. "Is she the one?"

"Yes."

"Jamal, she told me that she was one of the organizers and she didn't have to go through the security."

Releasing a low growl, Jamal thought about firing the man on the spot, but he could understand how Lucy had fooled him. "Everybody goes through the metal detectors, no excuses. I don't care if it's the mayor, the president or the Pope."

Jamal headed back to where MJ was standing. He could see she was shaken up. "Come on, babe. I'm getting you out of here." He wrapped his arms around her shoulders and headed for the back exit.

MJ shook her head. "I'm still in shock right now."

Getting into his car, they headed for his place.

On the ride over to Jamal's house, Michael called Mimi and told her what happened at the park.

"My goodness. Brent and I are going to meet you guys at Jamal's."

They all pulled up at Jamal's place at the same time.

Brent hopped out of the car and gave MJ a tight hug. "That had to be some scary stuff. Are you all right?"

"I'm fine, thanks to this guy." She nodded to Jamal.

Mimi rushed over to Jamal and gave him a hug as well. "I knew you were a good dude underneath all that playboy exterior."

"I would do anything for the woman I love, including taking a bullet for her."

MJ crossed over to Jamal and kissed him slow and deep. "You don't know how thankful I am that you love me that much."

The group headed inside and settled in the sunroom. "I can't believe Lucy was that crazy." Brent shook his head.

"Are you sure it was just one date?" Mimi asked.

"So, I kissed her." Jamal shrugged his shoulders.

MJ raised her eyebrow. "One kiss and one date led this woman to stalk you and try to shoot us or you?"

Jamal held his hands up. "I don't know."

"I don't mean to make light of this situation, but can we get some food in here?" Mimi asked. They all broke into laughter.

"Let's feed Mimi." Jamal rose to his feet and headed to the kitchen. MJ followed him. Alone in the kitchen, Jamal pulled MJ into his arms.

"I was so scared out there." Jamal kissed her on the forehead. "If anything ever happens to you, I don't know what I'd do."

"You could've gotten hurt, too."

"And I would've gotten over that, but not losing you." Jamal smiled. "This is *not* the plan I had for the day."

"Yeah, we didn't even get to the Sunshine Café truck."

Jamal crossed over to his refrigerator and pulled out some cheese and cold cuts. He grabbed a beer for Brent and bottles of water for him, Mimi and MJ. "MJ, the food truck wasn't what I was thinking about." Facing her, he smiled. "I wanted today to be special. Wanted to celebrate your success with the event. Well, I'm sorry it was ruined."

"Jamal, we're still here and alive. Nothing was ruined." She grabbed the drinks as Jamal placed the cheese and cold cuts on a plate.

"Y'all better not be in there doing anything nasty around the food!" Mimi called out.

Shaking her head, MJ headed for the sunroom.

Chapter 18

The rest of the festival went off without any more incidents. Jamal made sure his staff followed all of the rules about security. MJ, however, didn't return to the festival, but she kept her eye on the reports about it.

By all accounts, everyone was having a good time. As she sat in her office, Michael was proud of what she'd done. Now she was preparing proposals for other clients. She was in high demand and she couldn't be happier. Since her staff had worked so hard on the jazz fest, she'd given them two days off.

"Knock, knock," Jamal said as he walked into MJ's office. "Where is everybody?"

"At the festival or at home. I gave everybody time off. I'm just getting new clients lined up."

"So we're all alone, huh?" Jamal closed the door and locked it.

"What are you doing?" Michael smiled, knowing what was coming next. Jamal crossed over to her.

"First, I'm going to take off all of your clothes." He was glad she was wearing a sundress. He slid the straps down her shoulders, exposing her smooth brown skin. The dress fluttered to the floor. MJ stood there in black lace underwear making him smile.

"So, what's next?"

Jamal responded by stripping down to his boxer briefs. Michael marveled at the sight of his chiseled body. Strong thighs, six-pack abs and muscular arms that always made her feel safe when she was wrapped up in them.

The evidence of his arousal made her mouth water. She reached for the waistband of his underwear and tugged them down. She stroked his hardness and Jamal groaned in delight. Dropping down to her knees, MJ took him into her mouth, licking and sucking him until he called out her name.

Just when he felt as if he was going to explode, MJ pulled back and Jamal lifted her up and dropped her on her desk. "Let me take those panties off." Jamal didn't slide them off; he just ripped the lace off then spread her thighs apart. He buried his face between her thighs, sucking and lapping her wetness until her thighs quaked. "Yes, Jamal! Yes!"

He deepened his kiss, sucking on her throbbing bud, and Michael exploded. She pushed him back in her chair then mounted him. Slowly, she ground against him. Jamal plunged deeper and deeper inside her.

"That's it, baby. Ride me."

MJ threw her head back while Jamal sucked her breasts, sending waves of pleasure up and down her spine. Her moans floated through the air as she reached her climax and collapsed against his chest. Their bodies were covered in sweat and their hearts shared the same beat.

"That was amazing," she whispered.

"You always are. God, I love you, woman."

Michael closed her eyes and let the warmth of his love wash over her. "We should get out of town."

"Great minds think alike. I was wondering if you wanted to go to Savannah with me next week. It's time for the Carver low-country boil."

"I'd love to go."

"We can make a vacation of it, stay for a week, hang out on Tybee Island and stay away from crowds."

MJ nodded. "That sounds heavenly."

"But tonight, we're going to find Hercules in the sky."

"Such a sexy nerd. I can't wait."

Epilogue

Savannah, Georgia.

MJ hadn't expected so many people at the Carver family low-country boil, even if it was Thanksgiving. She thought it would just be family members, not half the town. It was like a smaller version of the jazz festival. She stood back and drank in the crowd and the pots of seafood. Everyone was either cooking or serving plates to the older people who were seated at the wooden picnic tables. MJ had been in charge of the rice—serving it, anyway. Jamal's gran, Miss Ethel, had said she'd let MJ cook something next year.

"You have to earn a cooking slot here because we will let you know if your food is not up to par. You're the first one of Jamal's women to actually ask to help

out." The older woman had smiled at MJ. "I like you
a whole lot."

"Penny for your thoughts." Jamal wrapped his arms
around MJ's waist.

"Was thinking about your grandmother and what
I'm going to cook next year."

"You better mean it because she doesn't forget anything." MJ whirled around and faced Jamal. He was
cute in his red apron and chef's hat.

"Are all of these people your relatives?"

Shaking his head, Jamal explained what the low-
country boil was all about. It had started out as the
Carver family reunion, but then they had ended up with
so much food left over that they had to throw it out or
give it away. So, Ethel decided to invite the whole neighborhood. Those who could bring something would, but
everybody ate.

"Your grandmother is an amazing woman."

Jamal nodded then rubbed his nose against MJ's. "I
figured something out."

"What's that?"

"You're a lot like Gran. Smart, successful, won't take
no for an answer and very independent."

"Okay, sounds good to me."

"And here's something else that I realize. MJ, I can't
live my life without you." He dropped his hands from
her hips and got down on one knee. All eyes turned
to the couple and a few oohs and awws rose from the
crowd.

"Michael Jane, make me the happiest man in the
world and say you will marry me."

She brought her hand to her mouth as Jamal pulled a black velvet box from his pocket. "Oh, my God. I don't know what to say."

"'Yes' would be good."

"Yes, yes, of course I will marry you!"

Jamal lifted her into his arms and spun her around. The crowd broke out into applause as he kissed MJ long and deep. He knew that he'd found the only woman he'd ever need and he couldn't have been happier.

Written with permission...

When she said yes, a player died. When she said yes, he became the protector of one heart: hers.

A couple of years ago, my best friend was ready to give up on love. She'd let the wrong guy worm his way into her heart—despite my warnings. So when she finally let him go, I gave her some advice that a lot of you didn't like too much. I told her to rebound, have fun and not to take dating too seriously. Of course, at the time, I was taking dating too seriously. I have to say that I'm glad she didn't take my advice. She looked past his playboy exterior and saw his heart. And he was able to make her believe in love again. They danced around their feelings as if they were in a ballroom for a while, but when things got real, she said yes.

He took her home and introduced her to all of the important people in his family. And when he got down on one knee to propose, she said yes. So, you know what this means. This is the first Mis-Adventures Couple! Though I'd like to take credit for this wonderful

union, I'm not going to do that. I'm just going to wish them the best!
   XOXO-Mimi.

* * * * *

Want more of Cheris Hodges's sensual titles?
Check out her previous books:

MAKE YOU MINE AGAIN (featured in
       BLISSFUL SUMMER)
       FEEL THE HEAT

Available now from Harlequin Kimani Romance!

COMING NEXT MONTH
Available October 17, 2017

#545 TAMING HER BILLIONAIRE
Knights of Los Angeles • **by Yahrah St. John**
Maximus Knight is used to getting what he wants, so seducing gallery owner
Tahlia Armstrong into turning over her shares of his family's company should
be easy. But when a shocking power play threatens their passionate bond,
Tahlia must decide if she can trust Max with her heart.

#546 A TOUCH OF LOVE
The Grays of Los Angeles • **by Sheryl Lister**
After an explosion shattered Khalil Gray's world, café owner Lexia Daniels
becomes the only person he can't push away. The ex-model is happy to explore
their chemistry as long as it means resisting real emotion. But playing by his
old rules could cost him the love he never thought he'd find...

#547 DECADENT DESIRE
The Drakes of California • **by Zuri Day**
Life's perfect—except for the miles that separate
psychologist Julian Drake from his longtime love,
Nicki Long. So when the Broadway dancer returns
to their idyllic town, Julian is beyond thrilled. But
Nicki's up against a deadly adversary that could end
her future with the Drake of her dreams...

#548 A TIARA UNDER THE TREE
Once Upon a Tiara • **by Carolyn Hector**
Former beauty queen Waverly Leverve can barely
show her face in public after an embarrassing meme
goes viral. But business mogul Dominic Crowne
wants to sponsor Waverly in a pageant scheduled
for Christmas Eve. Can he help her achieve
professional redemption and find his Princess
Charming under the mistletoe?

Get 2 Free Books,
Plus 2 Free Gifts —
just for trying the
Reader Service!

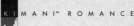

LOVE
Harlequin romance?

Join our Harlequin community to share your thoughts and connect with other romance readers!

Be the first to find out about promotions, news, and exclusive content!

Sign up for the Harlequin e-newsletter and download a free book from any series at

www.TryHarlequin.com

CONNECT WITH US AT:

Harlequin.com/Community

 Facebook.com/HarlequinBooks

 Twitter.com/HarlequinBooks

 Instagram.com/HarlequinBooks

 Pinterest.com/HarlequinBooks

ReaderService.com

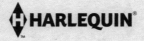 **HARLEQUIN®**

ROMANCE WHEN YOU NEED IT

HSOCIAL2017

Need an adrenaline rush from nail-biting tales
(and irresistible males)?

Check out **Harlequin® Intrigue®**
and **Harlequin® Romantic Suspense** books!

New books available every month!

CONNECT WITH US AT:

Harlequin.com/Community

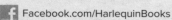 Facebook.com/HarlequinBooks

Twitter.com/HarlequinBooks

 Instagram.com/HarlequinBooks

Pinterest.com/HarlequinBooks

ReaderService.com

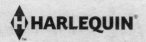 **HARLEQUIN®**

**ROMANCE WHEN
YOU NEED IT**

SGENRE2017

Looking for inspiration in tales
of hope, faith and heartfelt romance?

Check out **Love Inspired**®,
Love Inspired® **Suspense** and
Love Inspired® **Historical** books!

New books available every month!

CONNECT WITH US AT:

www.LoveInspired.com

Harlequin.com/Community

 Facebook.com/LoveInspiredBooks

 Twitter.com/LoveInspiredBooks

www.ReaderService.com